Lasso

SAMMIE WARD

Dedication

To Betty, I am forever grateful for all of the love, support, and being there. Thanks a million, little sister.

Chapter One

"Dr. Phillips, what do you want me to do with all of the messages from Dr. Thorpe?"

Chloe Dutch, the medical support assistant for the orthopedic clinic, asked. She held up a stack of papers.

"You can throw them in the trash can for all I care," Nikki answered.

"What? Why?" Nurse Corina Eggleton asked, a look of confusion on her face. "What did he do this time?"

Nikki didn't answer.

"He said it was urgent," Chloe replied. "Maybe you should call him back."

"Mind your business," Nikki replied. She snatched the messages from Chloe's hand. She rushed into her office and slammed the door behind her. She didn't bother reading them and tossed them in the trash can. Dr. Winston Thorpe had nothing she wanted to hear.

Nikki paced to and fro, twisting the two-carat diamond engagement ring on her finger. Winston had been calling, leaving voice and text messages, since she'd walked out on him last night.

The cellular phone in her white lab coat vibrated. She looked at it and read another text message from Winston. *We have to talk.*

She deleted it. "Talk? We don't have to talk," she said to herself. "You said everything you needed to say last night when you told me that you were not ready to marry me."

Nikki walked around her desk and sat in the large chair. She tossed her red headband on the desk. Morning rounds were going on; she had to get herself together. She couldn't believe her five-year relationship with Winston had come to this. How did they get here? She still couldn't wrap her mind around all that had transpired in the past twenty-four hours. All she knew was that she and Winston had been arguing nonstop the past couple of months. It seemed they were drifting further and further apart. Dr. Nichole Phillips and Dr. Winston Thorpe were considered the ideal couple. Both were smart, attractive, and successful. Both were orthopedic surgeons. Everyone thought they looked good together and knew one day they would be announcing their wedding day. They'd met at Duke University, Durham, North Carolina, School of Medicine. It was her first day of her residency when Winston walked into her exam room by mistake. She didn't mind. For Nikki, it was love at first sight as her hazel eyes took in all five feet ten inches of him.

Winston smiled. Her heart dropped into her stomach. "I'm sorry, I didn't know anyone was here."

"That's all right," the female patient said. "Are you my doctor?" she asked him, looking him up and down.

Winston's brown eyes locked with Nikki's. "No. It seems like you have the best doctor in…" He looked down at her name tag. "Dr. Phillips. I'm sure she will take good care of you."

"Thank you, Dr…" Nikki stole a look at his name. "Thorpe."

"It's no problem, Dr. Phillips, but if you need help, I'll be in the room next door."

Nikki watched him until the door closed behind him.

"He was yummy," the female patient squealed. "Wow. He can examine me anytime."

Nikki didn't answer. She nodded in agreement. She hoped to run into Dr. Thorpe again.

The next morning, Nikki got her wish. On her way to get breakfast, she was waiting for the elevator. The doors opened. Winston and three other residents were getting off on her floor. Their eyes met. He smiled.

"Good Morning, Dr. Phillips," he said in a warm tone.

Nikki decided to play it cool, but seeing him again, she felt butterflies in her stomach. "Good morning, Dr. Thorpe. It's good to see you again."

"Same here," Winston said. "Where are you headed?"

"I'm about to grab breakfast."

"How about I accompany you." Winston made a U-turn and got back on the elevator.

"It's time to start rounds," Dr. Morris added.

"Cover for me," Winston said. "I'll be right back."

"Look—" Dr. Morris began.

"I covered for you yesterday," Winston reminded him. He pointed at him. "You owe me."

"Ten minutes," Dr. Morris answered then followed the other doctors into the clinic.

Winston glanced at Nikki. "We're on our first date."

Nikki leaned back. "Date? It's the hospital cafeteria for breakfast. I don't consider that a date."

Winston pushed the down button. "Then we need to do something about that, don't we?"

Nikki smiled to herself as she recalled their first real date. Winston had taken her to Le Bouche, an upscale French restaurant in Washington, D.C. It was the first of many nights there for them, and also where he'd proposed to her.

In the beginning, everything between them was beautiful. Nikki continued turning the ring on her finger. She guessed it was how all relationships started—flowers, candy, fancy restaurants, and hours of hot, steamy sex. They couldn't get enough of each other. Inseparable. When you saw one, you saw the other. These days they couldn't be in the same room five minutes without fighting. How had things changed between them so much?

Nikki stood. She strolled over to the window, looking out at the D.C. skyline. The Washington Monument stood in the distance. She loved this city and hoped to settle down here with Winston. Now she wasn't sure that was going to happen.

"You can't go in there!" Nikki heard Chloe exclaim.

The door flew open. Nikki found herself staring in the face of her fiancé, Dr. Winston Thorpe.

* * *

"I left you a dozen messages," Winston snapped. "Why didn't you call me back?"

"Call you back? Why would I do that?" Nikki fired back. "You said everything you needed to say last night," she emphasized. "There's nothing left for us to discuss." She walked over to her desk and sat down hard in the chair.

Winston looked down at the floor. He stuck both of his hands in his white hospital coat. "Why are you acting like this, Nikki?"

Nikki jumped to her feet. "You know why."

"No. I don't," Winston said. "Enlighten me."

"Are you going to play dumb?" Nikki asked. "I'm not playing," Winston said.

"So, you are dumb?" Nikki threw back. She noticed a twitch at his lower jawline. He was trying his best to remain calm. She'd hit a nerve.

"See, there you go," Winston pointed out. "That mouth of yours. You never think before you speak. Last night, you ran out of the apartment. We didn't get a chance to finish talking. We have been together too long to play games."

"Yes, we have," Nikki said, coming from around the desk. "So why don't you tell me what brought about this new attitude about marriage? We talked about getting married; you proposed to me."

"I know I did."

"Then what?"

"Why don't we meet later? I will drop by your place after work, and we will finish talking."

"Tell me now," Nikki insisted.

"This isn't the time or place," Winston said.

Nikki couldn't help the ominous feeling flowing through her. Winston was unable to look her in the eyes. Something was going on. He was hiding something. She didn't like feeling left out.

"It's as if you have bad news," Nikki said. "Why won't you tell me now?"

"Because I do not want to discuss it here."

"Then why did you come?"

"Because you wouldn't answer my calls or my texts, and I wanted to see if you were all right."

"I hate it when you do this," Nikki exclaimed. "I can take it, whatever it is. Good news. Bad news." She was on the verge of tears. "Just tell me!"

"I don't want to hurt you," Winston said. "Last night I..." His voice trailed off.

Nikki closed her eyes. She had a feeling what he had to tell her was going to be bad.

Winston clasped his hands together; she could see hurt written all over his face. What he was trying to tell her was difficult. She was even more uncomfortable.

"There is no easy way to say this, Nikki, so I'll just say it."

"Winston. You are scaring me. Just tell me, please."

"It's over, Nikki," he spat out.

The words hit her like a ton of bricks. She stumbled back. Her mouth gaped. She couldn't believe what she was hearing. It explained the reason he hadn't wanted to discuss marriage. He was dumping her.

"Bastard. We have been together five years." Nikki placed a hand to her chest. "Five years I have invested in this relationship, and now you're telling me it's over. Without warning. Without a reason."

"What about me?" Winston threw back. "You're not the only one that invested in this relationship. I have also given my time and energy. I can't do it anymore."

Nikki sniffed. "You can't do it anymore. That's rich."

"You are making me out to be the bad guy," Winston said. "In case you haven't noticed, we haven't been getting along. Arguing nonstop."

"Winston, all couples go through rough patches," Nikki replied. "But they work through them. They don't just call it quits."

"We are way past that, and I think you know it," Winston answered. "We have been growing apart the past couple of years, but the last six months have been the roughest. It's time to end this."

This?" Nikki repeated in disbelief. She couldn't believe how arrogantly and nonchalantly he referred to what they had. "You called it a 'this'?"

"There is more." Winston cast his eyes down. "Much more." Nikki gave him a look of disdain. What was he going to tell her next? He'd fathered a child? He was married. Gay? "What else could there be?"

Winston took a deep breath. "I'm getting married," he mumbled. "To someone else."

Nikki felt like someone had kicked her in the solar plexus. She snapped her mouth shut. "Wait. What? Did you just say you were marrying someone else?" She covered the small space between them. "Who the hell are you marrying?"

"You don't know her," Winston quickly added. "She's a friend of the family."

Nikki placed her hands on her hips. "Which family? Yours? They know we are together. Why would they?"

"My family never liked you," Winston said.

Nikki blinked. "This is the first I have heard of it."

Winston tilted his head to one side. "I never told you."

"Oh really? Looks like there are a lot of things you never told me," Nikki exclaimed.

"The wedding is next week," Winston managed to get out.

Nikki rocked in her pumps. "Next week?" Her head was spinning. She was telling herself that this wasn't happening.

Maybe she was being punked. Because there was no way that the man she loved for the past five years would tell her he was getting married in a week to another woman.

She swallowed the lump in her throat. "You're standing there telling me that you are marrying another woman next week? Who is it? Be a man and tell me who it is right now!"

"Fine, if you want to know," Winston barked. "It's Aliessa Coffer."

Nikki tilted her head to one side. She was sure she'd heard the name before, but she couldn't remember where. "Wait a moment." It was as if a lightbulb went off in her head. "Isn't she the daughter of the Bartholomew Coffer that is on the board of directors for the hospital?"

"Yes, that is the one," Winston said. "Her father is the CEO of Dandelion Pharmaceuticals."

Nikki's heart dropped into her stomach. She remembered where she heard the name Aliessa Coffer—her name was always mentioned in the society section, and the paparazzi followed her all around D.C. She was a successful art buyer who owned a trendy gallery. She remembered Winston taking her to a couple of exhibits. She couldn't help but think maybe that was where they met or maybe were meeting each other. Why wouldn't he? She was beautiful, rich, younger, and now she was becoming Dr. Winston Thorpe.

"You bastard!" Nikki exclaimed.

"Keep your voice down," Winston hissed. "People will hear you."

"I don't care," Nikki yelled. "The staff should know what kind of asshole you are." Tears that she was holding back began to fall. "How could you do this to me?"

Winston stepped forward. Nikki stepped back. "I'm sorry, Nikki. I didn't plan for any of this to happen; it just did."

"How long?" Nikki clenched her fist. "How long have you been seeing her?"

"Why?" Winston asked. "What good will it do for you to know?"

"I asked you how long," Nikki replied. She was trying her best to act like a lady, but looking at him, she wanted to punch him in the face.

Winston closed the small space between them. "Nikki, let me—"

Nikki's hand found the right side of his face.

Winston closed his eyes. "I'm so—"

Nikki found his face again. She wanted to kill him.

"I deserved that," Winston said.

"Damn right." She raised a hand to hit him again.

Winston caught her hand in midair. He placed it in a vise grip. "I know you are hurt. But let's be adults about this."

Nikki dropped to a crouching position as if she had been hit in the stomach. She let out a loud wail.

"Nikki, please don't."

A moment later, the door opened and Dr. Patrick Penn rushed in with a bewildered expression on his face. "What is going on in here? The staff, not to mention the patients, can hear you all the way down the hall. This is a hospital."

Embarrassed and devastated, Nikki rushed out past Dr. Penn. She rushed down the hall and out of the clinic. "Nikki!" she heard Winston calling behind her.

Several hours later, Nikki let herself inside the apartment.

She didn't remember how long she'd sat in her vehicle. She returned to the clinic only for Dr. Penn to urge her to take the rest of the day off. He volunteered to cover the rest of her patients for her.

Nikki headed straight into her bedroom. She didn't bother removing her clothes. She threw herself across the queen size bed. Looking up at the ceiling, she felt wave after wave of despair wash over her. She flopped over onto her side. She grabbed and punched the pillow over and over again. The thought that Winston had cheated and was marrying another woman was tearing her heart apart. She felt like her life was over.

* * *

BAM! BAM! BAM! Nikki heard the loud knocking through a foggy haze. She glanced over at the clock. It was 4:00 p.m. It had only been three hours. She didn't remember dozing off. She stretched an arm over her head.

"Nikki! You'd better open this door," she heard David Combs yell. A good friend since medical school, David was a classmate to both her and Winston. A fellow orthopedist, David was a hand specialist.

"I know you're in there," David said, resting on the doorbell.

He knocked again.

Nikki threw her long legs over the side of the bed. On wobbly knees, she made her way to the door and opened it.

She came face to face with a bewildered David, and next to him was Corina. Both were wearing worried expressions on their faces. They brushed past Nikki.

"Are you okay?" David asked. He threw his hands up in a surrendering gesture. "That's a stupid question."

"We stopped by to see how you were," Corina said. "To see if you need anything."

Nikki walked over and sat on the sofa. She folded one leg under the other. "Don't worry," she answered in a somber tone. "I'm all right."

David sat next to her. Corina sat in the chair across from them. Nikki ran a hand through her hair. "I'm...I'm still in shock. I never saw it coming. How could I not know there was another woman?" She was babbling. "I didn't see the signs. Nada. Nothing. I know we were arguing more than usual the last couple of months but still I...I..." Her voice trailed off.

"Never thought," Corina finished for her.

"He's getting married," Nikki continued. "Can you believe it? I waited for his sorry ass five years, and he had the nerve to tell me he's marrying someone else. Someone whose younger and richer." She was seething with anger and humiliation. "I guess I couldn't get him where he wanted to go."

"Yeah, like running the hospital," Corina said.

"It hurts." Nikki drew her legs together. She laid her head on her knees. "How could he?" She started crying again. "How could he?"

"Maybe it's for the best," David said.

"Dr. Combs," Corina exclaimed. She moved next to Nikki and placed an arm of comfort around her. "Can't you see she's devastated? Don't pay attention to him. He's a man. What does he know?"

David flashed Corina a look. "I know that was stupid," he murmured. "I apologize."

Corina returned his look with one of her own. She refocused on Nikki. "When did sorry ass say he's getting married?"

11

Nikki wiped the tears on the sleeves of her shirt. She sniffed. "Next week."

"Next week?" Corina repeated. She handed Nikki a tissue from the box on the end table.

"Who knows how long he has been seeing her." Nikki dabbed at her eyes.

"Winston isn't the type to do anything without thought," David said, then, looking at the women's expressions, wished he'd kept his mouth shut.

"You mean, Winston isn't the type to do anything that doesn't benefit Winston," Corina replied.

"He isn't like that," Nikki defended.

Corina's mouth gaped. "You're defending him?"

Nikki looked away. She couldn't believe that she was protecting him. She looked at the wall as if she could find the answer to her dilemma written there.

"Winston humiliated you. He broke up with you in front of the entire clinic," Corina explained. "By now I'm sure it's all over the hospital, and you're defending him."

Nikki sniffed. "Go ahead. Make me feel more humiliated than I already am." She laid her head on Corina's shoulder.

"I wasn't trying to do that," Corina said, giving her friend a hug. She focused on David. "You're quiet."

"I received an invitation to the wedding," David said nonchalantly.

Nikki's head popped up. Corina gave David a look that could kill.

"Why are you staring at me like that? I didn't say I was going."

"You knew?" Nikki launched from the sofa. "Didn't you?"

"He knew," Corina chimed in. "That's his boy." She folded her arms across her chest. "I know men."

"You mean you hate men," David replied.

"Only the ones that are two-timing cheats and their friends that cover for them," Corina said.

David stood. He stuck his hands into his pockets and rocked on the heels of his suede loafers. "I knew. I found out a month ago. I wanted to tell you but didn't know how."

"What do you mean, you didn't know how?" Nikki exclaimed. "You just open your mouth and tell me."

"It's not that simple," David replied.

On one hand, Nikki felt sorry for David. She was sure he was in a perplexing predicament. He was a friend to both her and Winston. It must have been hard for him to keep something like that from her. She didn't want to lose a friend. But on the other hand, she was furious. He should have told her.

"David, how could you keep something like that from me?" she yelled. "I'm your friend." Her voice choked. "At least I thought I was."

"You are, Nikki," David tried to reassure her. He shook his head. "I just couldn't tell you."

"Couldn't?" Nikki inquired "Or wouldn't?"

"That's not fair. You don't know how many times I wanted to tell you."

"That's not good enough, David," Nikki said. "If you cherished our friendship, you would have told me. Instead, you made me look like a fool."

David leaned back in surprise. He blinked. "What? What are you saying?"

Nikki marched over to the door and yanked it opened. "I am saying that I want you to leave."

"Now wait a minute, Nikki," David protested. "I know you are upset—"

"You heard her, Dr. Combs," Corina echoed. "She asked you to leave."

David's face fell. "Fine. If that is the way you want it."

"I do," Nikki said. "Get out!"

Without another word, David turned on his heels and strolled out the door.

"Some friend he turned out to be," Corina said.

✱ ✱ ✱

"I had to get you out of the house," Corina said a week later. "I refuse to let you wallow in pity."

"Is that why you have dragged me to every antique store in town?" Nikki picked up a vase. "All of this is not necessary. I'm fine."

Corina took the vase from Nikki and picked up a green ashtray. She frowned. She put it back and moved over to an antique desk. "No, you're not. I haven't heard or seen you all week. You haven't been to work, answered any of my calls or texts. I was beginning to get worried, so I showed up on your doorstep."

"You embarrassed me by laying on the doorbell."

"I wasn't leaving until you opened the door." Corina waved a well-manicured finger at Nikki. "In time you will get over Winston, and one day you will meet the right man for you, someone that is caring, loving, and who will appreciate you for the beautiful and intelligent black woman that you are."

Nikki sniffed. She was still heartbroken over the breakup. "I wish I was as optimistic as you are."

Corina opened the top desk drawer. "All in due time, my sistah." She cast her a worried glance. "I'm glad you decided to take the week off to rest. It is a start to the rest of your life."

"You call this resting?" Nikki flipped the switch on the antique lamp atop the desk.

Corina put an arm around her waist. She gave her a tight squeeze. "That's what friends are for. I can't let you stay cooped and feeling sorry for yourself."

"I'm thinking of returning to work," Nikki announced. "I have to keep busy. Keep my mind off Winston."

"When are you thinking of returning?" Corina asked.

"Tomorrow," Nikki replied. "The sooner the better."

"Nikki, the wedding is Saturday," Corina said. "Why not wait until after it is over? They are going on a two-week honeymoon," she said. "Dr. Penn is fine covering your patients."

"You spoke with Dr. Penn?" Nikki asked in a surprised tone.

Corina smiled. "Don't look so shocked. Everyone in the clinic cares about you. They are all on your side. Whatever you need to do to get your head straight, we are behind you one hundred percent."

"I know," Nikki said. "That's why I need to be working and not lounging on my sofa. I just lay there and think about Winston and his socialite. I still did not get an answer to why he cheated. I want to know. I need to know."

Corina decided on the desk. She waved the sales clerk over.

She paid for it and set up a delivery date.

Thirty minutes later, they stepped out into the bright sunshine. It was humid. Nikki shield her eyes with her hand. The temperature was in the high eighties.

Both put on a pair of shades.

"He cheated," Corina said. "Why do you want to know? Will that change anything?"

"I don't know," Nikki said. "Maybe I just want to know what I did wrong. Why he felt like he had to go outside the relationship." She sighed. "I never saw it coming. I thought we were okay." She locked her arm in her friend as they strolled casually along the sidewalk. "We've been arguing a lot lately, but all couples do. They don't just throw everything away. Five years, Corina. Five years."

"I know. You still love him," Corina said. "But you did nothing wrong. What happened, Nikki, wasn't your fault. Don't beat yourself up over it. That's why I think you need to take some more time off. Go on vacation. Recharge yourself."

"Recharge myself?"

Corina laughed. "You do remember what the term means? When was the last time you took a vacation?"

"Vacation?" Nikki repeated.

"Yes. Vacation. When was the last time you took one?" Corina repeated.

Nikki's mind went to Winston. The last time they'd taken a trip together. It was three years ago. They decided to go skiing in Colorado. They enjoyed the snowy slopes during the day but did things to make the bearskin rug blush at night.

"Three years ago," Nikki said.

"You are long overdue," Corina said. "I think it's time to call a travel agent."

* * *

Later that day, Corina dropped Nikki off in front of her apartment building. Nikki refused Corina's offer to escort her to the door. She strolled into the elevator and rode to the fifth floor. She exited, walking the short hallway to number 505.

As soon as she slipped the key into the lock, her cell phone began to ring. She quickly unlocked the door and rushed into the living room. The phone continued ringing. Nikki reached down inside her large bag and pulled out her phone. She glanced at the number. It was her mother, the last person she wanted to speak to. Her mother was persistent; if she didn't answer, she would continue to call.

Sophie Phillips was a very loving and caring woman to everyone in the small town of Montgomery, Texas, but when it came to her one and only daughter, she was meddlesome and overbearing. Everything had to be her way or no way. Nikki loved her mother; they got along well, as long as they were not in the same town and spoke to each other as little as possible.

Nikki took a deep breath and answered the call. "Hello, Mother." She set the bag on the dining-room table. "How are you?"

"What took you so long to answer?"

"I'm just coming in the door, Mother. What can I do for you?"

"Do you have to answer like that?"

"Mother, I am not in the mood." Nikki wanted her mother to get to the reason she'd phoned. She was sure Winston had informed her that their relationship was over.

"Can't a mother call to see how her daughter is doing?"

"Most mothers, yes." Nikki headed into the bedroom. She sat down on the edge of the bed. While juggling the phone, she removed one clog and then the other. "But you, no. You spoke to Winston."

"How are you doing, dear?" her mother said in a soft tone. "I'm so sorry."

Just as Nikki thought, her mother had spoken to Winston. "How do you think I am, Mother?" Nikki inquired. "We were going to get married."

Sophie cleared her throat. "I know you are disappointed. But in time, you will forget about Winston and meet someone new."

"He never should have told you," Nikki said. "I'm sure you are ecstatic; you never cared for Winston."

"I am not ecstatic. Why would I be?" Sophie said. "That is the most ridiculous thing I have ever heard you say. Why didn't you tell me?"

"Because I didn't want to hear 'I told you so.'"

"I wouldn't have said that," Sophie said.

"I know you, Mother," Nikki said. "Whenever you get a chance, you love to tell me I am wrong, and you are right."

"That's because I usually am," Sophie boasted.

Nikki bit her lips. "That's why I didn't tell you."

"Nikki, you can think whatever you like. I am tired of putting up with your condescending and nasty attitude. Think what you want."

"I think you want to run my life. I'm in control, not you."

"Yes," Sophie snapped. "You are in control and look where that got you—dumped by your fiancé. He's marrying someone else."

"It's true. I was dumped," Nikki admitted. "I'm hurt. I'm going through a difficult time. You're my mother; you're supposed to call to offer words of encouragement, and not kick me while I am down."

"That is why I called, not to argue," Sophie said. "I want you to come home, spend time with your father and me."

Nikki rolled her eyes toward the ceiling. The last thing she wanted to do was spend time with her parents. It had been five years since her last visit to Montgomery, Texas. As far as she was concerned, that wasn't long enough. "No. I can't," Nikki said. "I'm busy. I have a heavy schedule at work," she lied.

Silence fell between them.

"I understand," her mother finally said. "If you change your mind, we miss you and want to see you." She ended the call.

* * *

"I think you should go," Corina said the next day as they met for lunch. The weather in late March was damp, breezy, and rainy. Flowers were blooming but today the sun had managed to break through. People were taking advantage of it, rushing in and out of the trendy shops in downtown, Washington, D.C.

"You don't know my parents," Nikki said as they strolled into a coffee shop.

"We can't choose our parents." Corina said. "None are perfect and all have issues. Yours is no different. But five years is a long time not to visit them. I'll have a caramel macchiato," she said to the cashier.

"I don't think it's long enough. I'll have a white-chocolate mocha."

Corina gave Nikki a look of concern. "That's nothing to brag about."

"Who's bragging? It's frustrating and drives me crazy. My mother has this 'always right' attitude; my dad never stands up to her." Nikki accepted the coffee, paid, and thanked the cashier. She led the way to a booth next to the window.

"Did something happen the last time you were home?" Corina took the seat across from her.

"My mother and I had a big blow-up the last time I was home," Nikki answered.

"What was it about?"

"Me choosing a career."

"What about it?" Corina said. "I would think your parents would be proud to have a doctor in the family."

"My father is okay with it," Nikki replied. "My mother raised me to believe that I should get married, have babies, and take care of the home."

Corina took a sip. "I can't see you being Donna Reed."

"I'm not," Nikki replied. "But a lot of women in Montgomery are, including my mother."

"I thought you were from Houston."

"I'm from a small town called Montgomery. It's about a hundred miles outside of Houston. Population around twenty thousand," Nikki explained. "Cowboy country."

"Cowboy country," Corina replied. "You left it for the hustle and bustle of the city."

Nikki shrugged. "I wanted a different life. I fell in love. There are no cowboys in Montgomery."

"You stayed away because of Winston?"

Nikki nodded. "Yes. Winston."

"Any regrets?" Corina asked. "I mean, you could have been waking up every morning in the arms of a tall, hunky cowboy. Riding the wide-open spaces. Two or three little cowboys or cowgirls on your apron strings. But instead, you're working twelve to sixteen-hour shifts, on call at any given time, and performing nonstop surgeries. I could go on and on."

"Please don't. I love what I do."

Corina gave Nikki a quizzical look. "If I ask you something, do you promise not to get angry?"

Nikki returned the look. "It depends on what it is."

"Could it be that you don't want to go home because your mother was right? You're trying to save face?"

"No. That's not it."

"Are you sure?" Corina inquired. "I know you, and just like your mother, you don't like to be wrong."

"That is true, but I wasn't meant to be a cowgirl, either."

Chapter Two

"Next up is Ross Kincaid," the rodeo announcer said. "He is currently third in world standing. In the bull-riding competition, he has been an all-around champion for the past two years. Kincaid is the man to beat tonight."

A round of applause and whistles drowned out the rest of the announcer's sentence.

"Folks, Ross is in first place and has a chance to ride away with the twenty-five-thousand-dollar purse. All he has to do is stay on old Delila for eight seconds. Ross is no stranger to riding. He was born in a cowboy family. Yes, sir, riding is in his blood."

"I bet it is," a young woman said to her friend. They both giggled.

"I'd like to ride him," the other woman chimed in.

Ross threw his long legs over the saddle. The large, black cowboy hat moved up and down as he listened to instructions from his brothers, Junior and Blake.

"Delila is a tough ole girl," Blake said. He hit Ross in the chest. "You are tougher. You are a Kincaid."

"Just relax. Concentrate," Junior added.

Ross took a couple of deep breaths to calm the adrenaline pumping through his body. He'd ridden the bull hundreds of times, but still gets a little nervous each time. Three years ago, he'd suffered a spinal cord injury and been out for an entire season. He was lucky. The fall could have ended his career, or he could have been stomped to death. He'd known many riders who'd died on the rodeo circuit.

Tonight was a terrible night for bull riders. So far none of the riders had been able to stay on Delila for more than three seconds. He was determined to walk away with the prize.

The gate opened. Ross and Delila sprang into action. One hand gripped the reins, while the free hand held the pose, his head high and clear of his body. Eight seconds was all he needed. Eight seconds. Like the professional he was, Ross rode with balance, stamina, and pure nerves.

The buzzer sounded. The onlookers came to their feet in applause. Ross hit the ground with a thud. He rolled onto his side to make sure he would not get trampled by the two-thousand-pound animal. Bingo the Clown ran out and expertly coaxed her back to her stall.

Ross lay there a moment looking up at the lights. A slow grin spread across his pecan-colored face. He'd done it again. He just won his 19th rodeo event. He raised a clenched fist in the air in victory.

* * *

"Ross, you have to talk to the reporters for ten minutes," Clinton Storay, the rodeo promoter, begged. "The contract states that you have to be accessible to the media, which you have not honored." A cheap, unlit Cuban cigar hung from his lips. "What do you think I ought to do about that?"

Ross continued loading Bullet into the horse trailer. "Mr. Storay, you know how I feel about interviews."

"I know. But an interview with you is good for the competition and you. Look at it as free advertisement for RFK Ranch."

Ross let down the tail on the truck.

"You have won the Southern Invitational three times. You haven't done an interview or fan meet," Mr. Storay explained. "You owe it to the fans to—"

Ross cut him off. "Then you shouldn't take me not doing this one either to heart." He noticed a twitch at Mr. Storay's lower jaw. He was angry. "Does this mean I have worn out my welcome at the Southern Invitational?"

Mr. Storay said nothing.

"Then I'll see you in two weeks at the Sweet Bronco Invitational." Ross opened the door to his Ford Bronco and jumped behind the steering wheel. Junior and Blake slid in next to him.

"Aren't you afraid Mr. Storay could make things hard for you?" Junior said. "Doing interviews can't be that bad."

Ross looked over at his brother. "Have you ever done one?"

"Not recently," Junior answered.

"Then what would you know about it?" Ross snapped.

"I just meant—" Junior tried to interject.

"Drop it. I don't like doing interviews and Mr. Storay knows that." He turned the key in the ignition, double- checked the side and rearview mirror before backing out of the parking space. He proceeded to drive out of the lot.

"Ross is always in the paper," Blake chimed in. "He is the only African-American Cowboy to ever get sponsorship. The articles are always positive. Besides, him not doing interviews gives him a mysterious persona. I think it's going to be alright."

"I agree," Ross said as he pulled out onto Route 10 and headed south toward Norstrom, Texas.

Ross drove along in silence. He looked out at the wide-open spaces of farmland, crops, and windmills in the distance. He looked out the windshield at the sky. There wasn't a star to be found. He loved the country. He was born here. He would die here.

As the truck ate up the highway, he was happy to be heading home. The past three years, he was always on the road, traveling from state to state to compete. He managed to visit often, but it didn't take away the claustrophobic feeling he felt when he was away from RFK Ranch too long. The 2,500 acres were his haven. It offered him contentment. He enjoyed walking and riding the land. No other career compared to it.

He had won millions from competition. But the RFK Ranch boasted a healthy income from sales of bulls, cattle, sheep, and horses. Three years ago, the family opened a dude lodge on the property. Visitors could choose a log cabin equipped with fireplaces and private baths or they could rough it out in one of the tents under the Texas sky. The lodge offered early morning rides for an outdoor breakfast, trail rides on horseback, and cattle drives alongside real cowboys.

There was also fly-fishing and hiking. Guests could also experience a Western ride in a horse-drawn stagecoach. The dude lodge had proved to be a wise decision. Business has been very profitable.

Ross had achieved everything in life he needed or wanted, including winning his 19th rodeo. He'd been riding since the age of four, when his father had put him on his first horse. Thunder was a Quarter Horse born and raised on the ranch. He knew there was nothing else he wanted to do. He won his first competition when he was fifteen. He began bull riding when he was eighteen and never looked back. A third-generation competitor. All the Kincaid brothers were on the circuit, but none had been as successful as Ross.

Ross glanced at his watch. It was 8:30 p.m. He planned to make it home before midnight. There was no hurry. It wasn't as if he had a reason to rush. No one was waiting for him. He'd thought maybe there was, once, but it wasn't meant to be.

Ross and Hailey Foster met in high school. Her family purchased the Cannon Ball Farm located over the valley from RFK. They became friends. The relationship blossomed into something more in their senior year.

Away in college, he proposed. Hailey promised to wait for him. The wedding was to take place after graduation. The union would have brought about the largest merging of two of the biggest ranches in the county. But when he returned home, Hailey had married someone else and moved away.

Ross was devastated. He never received an explanation of what happened. The Fosters wouldn't talk about Hailey. They would only say that it turned out for the best for both of them. But the betrayal left him with emotional scars. He didn't want to be in a relationship and he didn't trust women. He vowed never to get his heart broken again.

$$* \; * \; *$$

Ross made a left turn and drove the two-mile winding road into the ranch. He glanced over at the horses grazing in the pasture. A minute later, the split-level Kincaid Manor came into view. He nudged Blake. Junior jumped out and made his way toward the house.

Blake followed. Ross drove the truck to the back of the barn and parked on the side of the stables.

"Need some help?" Ross turned to find a sleepy looking Blake. He was stretching and yawning.

"I thought you went inside." Ross strolled to the back of the horse trailer. He lowered the ramp. He unloaded Bullet, Midnight, Morning Dew, Giggles, and Chuckles.

"I couldn't let you unload them by yourself." Blake helped escort the animals into their stalls.

"Good job, Giggles." Ross gently tapped the Quarter Horse on the back. She neighed at him as if she understood what he was saying. "Your mother, Thunder, would be proud." He placed her inside, tied the rope to the post. "That's a good girl," he said lovingly. He kissed the horse on the nose. "Let's get you cleaned up." He proceeded to pick one hoof and then the other.

"You know, if you put that much energy into a real woman," Blake teased, "you wouldn't be grouchy all of the time."

"I trust Giggles," Ross answered. "I don't trust women."

"It's unhealthy," Blake argued. "It's a horse."

"Your date book is just overflowing with women."

Blake chuckled. "Well, yeah."

"Right," Ross said. "Then why are you still single?"

"Who says I am?" Blake led Bullet into the stall next to Giggles. "There you go, boy, next to your favorite filly." He laughed. "Even the horses are getting more action than you."

Ross began combing Giggles. "You're hilarious."

"Speaking of women," Blake began cleaning Bullet's hoof, "I ran into Lena yesterday."

Blake peeped over at Ross. He was working meticulously. "She wanted to know if you are attending Mr. Spaulding's sixty-fifth birthday party," Blake continued. "She said she sent you an invitation."

Ross didn't respond.

Blake took a deep breath. "I know you heard me."

"Yeah. I heard you," Ross finally answered. He continued brushing the horse.

"And?"

"And I would like to finish grooming the horses so that I can get some sleep," Ross replied. "Looks like it is just you and me. Junior skipped out on us again."

Blake wasn't swayed. "I hate it when you change the subject."

Ross swirled around. "I'm not changing the subject. I'm not going."

Blake looked dumbfounded. "Why not? Lena came all the way over here to personally invite you, and you're not going."

"Did I ask her to stop by?"

Blake folded his arms across his chest, his legs spread slightly apart. "You're a real piece of work, you know that?"

"What do you want me to do?" Ross said. "I don't want to lead Lena on," he explained.

"Oh, so you do know that Lena likes you."

Ross refocused on grooming Giggles. "Of course, I know. I'm not blind."

"I'm glad to hear it. Everybody knows Lena has been in love with you since she was a little girl. She would follow you around like a lost puppy," Blake said. "I don't want to see her hurt again. She never got over it when you…" His voice trailed off when he saw Ross glaring at him. "Never mind. Just consider it. I know it will make Lena happy to see you there, even if it is out of obligation."

Ross's shoulders slumped. He was aware of how Lena felt about him.

Lena Spaulding's family owned the Silver Spur Ranch. It wasn't as large as the RFK or the Cannon Ball, but with fifteen hundred acres, Harry Spaulding had managed to turn the property into one of the top five black ranches in Texas.

The Kincaid's and Spaulding's were close friends and neighbors. Lena's brother, Harper, was like family to him. He and Ross were on the circuit together, but a spinal cord injury had forced him to leave the rodeo. He had become a successful real estate agent and from time to time lent his voice to calling local events. But the scrawny little girl with braces who followed him around, confessing her love for him—he thought it was nothing more than a crush.

Lena was sixteen when she told him how she felt. He was ten years her senior. She was young and impressionable. He didn't want to hurt her feelings. He carefully explained she was too young for him and that he loved her like the little sister he'd never had. She wasn't put off. She promised that when she grew up and became a woman she would become his woman.

30

Six years had gone by; Lena insisted her feelings for him had not changed. She was still in love with him. Ross still felt the same; he still looked at her like a little sister.

"I'll think about it," Ross finally said. Blake's face split into a wide grin.

"I said I'll think about it," Ross replied. "I didn't say I was going."

"Well, that's better than a flat out no," Blake added.

"When is Mr. Spaulding's party?"

"It's this Saturday." Blake frowned. "You didn't even open the invitation?"

"Nope," Ross replied. "Why should I, when I have you?"

* * *

"Morning, Mr. Kincaid," Chuck Weathersby, the cook, greeted Ross the next morning as he took a seat at the dining room table. His father, Franklin Sr., and his brothers, Blake and Junior, were already eating breakfast.

"You're late," Franklin Sr.'s voice boomed.

Ross glanced at his watch. It was 4:40 a.m. "By only ten minutes."

"You know what I always say," Franklin Sr. said.

"You can do a lot in ten minutes," Blake finished for him as he shoved a spoonful of grits into his mouth.

"That's time wasted," the brothers mimicked in unison.

Franklin Sr. cleared his throat. "Saw you in the morning paper." He tossed the newspaper on the table. "When are you going to give up rodeo competitions?"

Ross opened the paper to see a photo of himself accepting the trophy and prize money. He folded the paper.

Chuck placed a plate full of scrambled eggs, French toast, and sausages in front of Ross. He ignored his father's comment and dug in eating. He hadn't gotten into bed until after 2:00 a.m. and had gotten up at 4:00. He was functioning on a couple of hours of sleep. There was a ton of work to do on the ranch. He wasn't in the mood to argue with his father about a subject that had been discussed a thousand times.

"Chuck, is there any coffee?"

"Yes, sir. I'll bring your usual cup right away," Chuck replied.

"Thank you," Ross said as the middle-aged man disappeared into the kitchen. "Dad, we've talked about this already." He began eating the eggs. "I'm not giving up the circuit."

"Why are you doing it?" Franklin Sr. inquired. "It's not like you need the money. You were the one that talked me into turning this place into a dude ranch. I did it. But that was because I was under the impression that you would be here to help me run it. You are never around."

Ross didn't miss the looks shared on his brothers' faces. They appeared to be hurt by their father's remarks. Junior and Blake worked their butts off when he was away from the ranch. They'd helped make RFK Ranch the success it was today.

"What are you saying, Dad?" Ross exclaimed. "I'm here now. When I'm not around, Junior and Blake do a good job of running RFK."

Chuck set a cup of hot, steaming coffee in front of him. "When is that?" Franklin Sr. inquired. "When they are not following you around?" He took a sip of orange juice.

Ross knew his father was right. The Southern Invitational was a two-day event. It was close to home, but it lasted the entire weekend. "They only attend the local shows."

Franklin Sr. slammed his fist on the table. "I'm not going to be around forever. I need to know my boys will be responsible enough to run this ranch."

"We are more than responsible," Ross said. "You know that."

"You call what you're doing responsible? Ross, you are thirty-one. The oldest. You are supposed to be setting an example for Junior and the young one here. You can't keep doing what you're doing. It's time to give up that dang rodeo while you are still able to. Settle down. Get married. Give this old man some grandbabies." He looked at his three grown sons. "I can't believe it; I have three boys. There hasn't been a woman in this house since your mother passed on ten years ago, and there are no grandchildren to carry on the Kincaid name."

"Dad, you warned us to be careful about the women we get involved with," Junior said. "Just doing what you told us."

"I'm still too young," Blake threw in, chewing on a piece of sausage. "Twenty-five is way too young to think of marriage and babies." He glanced across the table at his older brother. "Ross may be closer to making you a granddad than the rest of us."

Junior's eyes stretched. "What are you talking about?"

Ross gave Blake a hard look. "He doesn't mean nothing."

"Is he talking about Lena Spaulding?" Junior asked. "She has had a thing for Ross since she was a little girl."

"Lena is a lovely girl," Franklin Sr. replied. "She's already like part of the family. It would be a good match. It would also merge the Kincaid and Spaulding ranches. We can own this whole valley."

"We already own the valley. Can we talk about something else, please?" Ross finished his coffee. "It's time to get started. There's a lot of chores that needs tending to."

"At least think about it," Franklin Sr. suggested.

"There's no chance of that," Ross answered. He stood, pushed the chair back, and strolled over to the work cabinet. Ross opened a drawer and took out a pair of work gloves.

He removed his black Stetson from the rack and placed it on his head. "I'm headed out to feed the calves, check on the birthing, and the vaccinations."

"Mark and the other hands took care of the calves while you were away," Franklin Sr. said in a sarcastic tone.

"There's still a lot of work to do," Ross replied. "Like mucking the stalls, weaning the calves, and moving them into the pasture."

"We still have to check Sumner Well." Blake said. "Remember, Ross? You asked me to test the drainage before you left. It's going to need some digging."

Ross could tell Blake was trying to calm the storm between father and son. "Time to get at it." He stepped outside in the crisp morning air. It was still dark out. He released the long breath he'd been holding in. It was one thing for their father to be angry with him for competing, but to be condescending toward Blake and Junior was going too far.

"You know, Dad is only like that because he's worried about you," Blake said, standing next to Ross. "We all are."

"There's no reason to be concerned about me. I've been riding over fifteen years," Ross reminded Blake. "We all have."

"You think you are Superman, but even he had a weakness," Blake replied. "The body can only take so much. You know what the doctor said; if you take one more nasty fall like you did several years ago, you may never walk again."

Ross was sure the family was worried about him. He was doing what he loved. It would kill his spirit not to compete. It was in his blood. "I can't stop now."

"When will you stop?" Blake inquired. "When you're in a wheelchair?"

"I can't believe this is coming from you. We all compete."

"Yes, but Junior and I are not as competitive. It's like you have some death wish."

"I have been very careful."

"You call riding Delila being careful?" Blake pointed out. "She has crippled men and they were lucky."

Ross managed a chuckle. "I'm not afraid of Delila. I did win."

"The end justifies the means."

"I'm physically able to withstand the fall or Dr. Baker would not have cleared me to ride."

"I can only imagine how that conversation went," Blake added. "If nothing else you proved that you're still crazy."

They headed for the bunkhouse. The hired hands loud talking and laughing could be heard from the outside. As they were about to walk inside, the cow dogs, Fred and Lucy, came running up to them. Both dogs barked and jumped on them.

Ross kneeled down to Fred. "Hey, boy." He scratched him behind the ears. Excited, the dog wagged its tail. "Did you miss me, boy?" The dog barked. "I missed you, too. Hey, girl," he said to Lucy.

Head wrangler Tom Horner opened the door and they strolled inside. He had been with RFK Ranch for ten years. He knew the cattle business like the back of his hand. Ross trusted him.

Tom tipped his white Stetson toward Ross. "Mr. Ross. Mr. Blake."

"Morning, Tom," Ross said. "Looks like you took care of things around here while my brothers and I were away. Thank you."

"Aw now, Mr. Ross, there is no need to thank me," Tom said. "I was just doing my job. Besides, winning your nineteenth rodeo is much more important. I'm not surprised you won," he continued.

The rest of the hired hands mumbled in agreement. "Too bad Dad doesn't think the same," Blake said.

Tom's eyes stretched. "Aw shucks, I wouldn't worry. Mr. Frank Sr. don't mean nothing by it. He's a proud man."

"That's what I said," Blake boasted.

"That's right," Beau Champ, another hand, chimed in. "We all know how proud Mr. Frank Sr. is of you. When we go into town, he brags to everyone that will listen."

Laughter filled the bunkhouse.

"He ain't lying," Tom said, slapping Ross on the back. "When are you going for number twenty?"

"The Sweet Bronco Invitational is in two weeks in Houston," Ross said. "The prize money isn't as big as the Southern Invitational, but it's worth competing."

"I might join you in the Sweet Bronco Invitational," Beau said, hiking up his blue jeans over his belly. "It's been a minute since I competed, but I believe I can still ride."

"I think you should," Blake said in a sarcastic tone.

"An old coot like you ain't got no business riding in no rodeo," Tom hissed at Beau.

Beau became agitated. "What are you saying? I can still ride." He simulated roping a calf. "I still got the moves."

"Not according to Doc Baker," Tom replied. "Remember what he said. One more hit to that noggin of yours, and we will have to put you out to pasture." He made a gesture as if Beau were crazy.

Everyone laughed.

"So, this is where everyone is," a female voice said from the doorway. All heads turned to Lena Spaulding, dressed in straight-leg jeans and a red, short-sleeved shirt, with a matching bandana around her neck. A white hat sat upon her head. Her hair, pulled in a long ponytail, hung down her back. She looked more beautiful than ever at 5:00 a.m.

The hired hands spoke, tilting their hats to Lena on the way out the door. Everyone knew how Lena felt about Ross.

"Boss, we'll get started on those daily chores," Tom said, bringing up the rear.

"I'll see you in a few minutes," Ross said.

"Good morning, Ross," Lena said when the coast was clear. She looked at her crush, smiling from ear-to-ear.

"Lena," Ross said dryly. "What brings you here so early in the morning? Hell, I don't think the rooster has even crowed yet."

Lena moved further into the room. "I wanted to catch you before you began your chores. I wanted to congratulate you on winning the Southern Invitational Rodeo, and to give you this." From behind her back, she presented a copy of the Norstrom Gazette. "Today's front page news." Excited, she began reading. "Local Cowboy Captures Nineteenth."

Ross took the copy of the paper and reread it. He handed it back to her. He didn't have the heart to tell her that he'd already seen it. "I hate that picture."

"I bought all of the copies at the stand. The article is going in my scrapbook with the others," Lena boasted.

"You have a scrapbook?"

"Of course," Lena replied. "I have all of your clippings from the past ten years."

Ross did not want to admit it, but he was touched. "The second reason I stopped by is that I wanted to know if you will be stopping by Daddy's birthday party this Saturday."

Ross didn't miss the look of anticipation on Lena's face. Blake was right; if he didn't show, Lena would be hurt. That was the last thing he wanted to do. "I'll be there."

She clasped her hands in excitement. "Great, we're going all out for Daddy's sixty-fifth birthday. I know Harper will be glad to see you. He was just saying the other day that it's been a while since he's laid eyes on you."

"Well, tell him I'm looking forward to catching up with him," Ross replied. "I'd better get to those chores." He nonchalantly guided her by the elbow toward the door. "I'll walk you out."

"How as the bull ride?" Lena asked.

"What do you mean?" He opened the door and escorted her outside. "You were there. I won."

They stood in front of the bunkhouse. Junior and Blake were helping some of the men repair a fence.

"Make sure you continue to listen to Dr. Baker," Lena said.

Ross's face clouded. "I don't need you to tell me what to do."

"I'm not telling you what to do," Lena defended. "It was just a suggestion."

"I'll see you at the party," Ross replied before stomping off toward the stables. He strolled inside, grabbed Bullet, and led him back outside. He needed to ride to clear his head. It was only five in the morning, and he was already having a bad day.

"Where are you off to?" Junior inquired.

"Figured I'd head over to the Sumner Well and check it out," Ross answered.

"There's nothing wrong with that well," Junior said. "The men already took care of it."

"It never hurts to take a second look."

"Do you want me to ride with you?" Junior asked.

"No. Take some of the men and finish vaccinating the new calves," Ross instructed. "Don't forget to muck out the stalls."

"I'll get right on it," Junior said. He nervously shuffled from one foot to the other. "Uh."

Ross glanced alongside Junior's head. The younger brother looked away. "You have something you wanna say?"

"Lena," Junior began.

"What about her?" Ross climbed on Bullet.

"She looked hurt when she left here."

"So?" Ross threw at him.

"Is that all you have to say?" Junior asked.

Ross pushed the black Stetson back on his head. "Why is it that everybody is in my business?" He gave a slight tug on Bullet's reins and galloped off. He hoped the rest of the day would be less eventful.

Chapter Three

The sounds of old school music flowed through Cadence's speakers during happy hour at the club. The mature crowd of men and women stood together in clusters, drinking and chatting. A few brave couples graced the dance floor, hand dancing and busting old moves. The club was crowded as usual. Good food, music, and the energetic atmosphere kept the regulars returning.

"Nikki, slow down on the drinks," Corina scolded. "That's your fifth. You're not a drinker and you didn't eat anything at dinner."

"I'm all right," Nikki said in slurred speech. She hiccupped. "Oops." She covered her mouth with a hand and giggled.

Corina placed a hand to her head. "You're drunk."

"I'm not drunk." Nikki hiccupped again. "But I'm feeling good." The waiter, Cory passed by with a drink tray. She attempted to grab a glass.

"Oh no, you don't." Corina slapped her hand away. "You have had enough." She dismissed Cory. "I'm taking you home."

Corina attempted to stand Nikki on her feet, but she pulled away. "Let me go." She stumbled and headed toward the bar. "I want another drink."

"No. No." Corina grabbed her arm and headed toward the front of the club.

As they were leaving, Winston and several doctors from the hospital were coming in. Nikki was a little drunk, but she would know the face of that good-for nothing scumbag anywhere. She hadn't seen him since he'd dumped her. She'd rehearsed what she was going to say to him when she ran into him. She couldn't think of a better time than now to let him have it.

Nikki staggered toward him. "Well, if it isn't that good for nothing, low down, dirty scumbag Winston Thorpe."

Winston blinked. "Nikki, what are you doing here?"

Nikki weaved. She saw two of him and pointed at both. "That's a stupid question. I've been drinking."

Winston stepped back, looking her up and down. "You're drunk."

Nikki staggered. Corina grabbed her arm to steady her. "That's right. I'm drunk. I am feeling no pain. No pain in my heart right now." She hit herself repeatedly in the chest. "You cheated on me." She hiccupped. The doctors in the group began whispering among themselves.

"You don't know what you're talking about."

"I do know!" Nikki exclaimed. "You cheated on me and got her pregnant, and now you are marrying her."

Embarrassed, Winston glanced around. A small crowd had gathered to see what the commotion was all about. He looked like he wanted to hide in a hole. "I dropped you because you are a cold, psychotic bitch."

"What?" Nikki responded. "Cold and psychotic? Why, you—" She launched toward him, but Corina and several of the doctors managed to subdue her.

"See what I mean," Winston said. "The woman is crazy."

Nikki attempted to kick Winston but missed. The sudden movement caused the alcohol to rush to her head. She felt dizzy.

"She's not in her right mind," Corina chimed in. "You led her on for years with promises of marriage, then when a rich meal ticket came along, you dumped her and told her a week before the wedding."

"That's low," a woman on the sideline said.

"Leave his sorry ass," another woman said.

"You can do better," a husky male voice screamed out.

"No. No, she can't," Winston bragged. "I'm a doctor."

"So," a group of women shouted. "That just makes you a sorry-ass doctor."

"She's a doctor, too," Corina replied.

"I don't have to listen to this," Winston said. He attempted to sidestep Nikki.

All of the bottled-up aggression Nikki had held back rushed to the surface and she jumped on Winston's back. She punched him repeatedly in the head. Winston covered up as best he could; he easily flipped her off his back. She landed on the floor with a thud.

Winston's eyes glared down at her. He raised a hand to hit her. Corina jumped in front of her to protect her. The onlookers groaned in disapproval. Winston dismissed her with a wave of his hand. "The bitch is crazy." He proceeded into the club.

Corina helped Nikki to her feet. "I know you want to get back at him. What were you thinking, confronting him like that?"

"When I saw his ugly face," Nikki said, "I just wanted to smash it in. The bastard."

"Do you feel better?" Corina helped her outside.

The cool, crisp spring night air helped Nikki sober up a little. Her head was still spinning. She was going to have one heck of a hangover. But it would be worth it, knowing she'd gotten a small measure of revenge.

The two women walked down the sidewalk toward overflow parking. They stopped at the corner, waiting for the light. Nikki looked across the street. She thought she saw what looked like Winston's Mercedes Benz. She adjusted her eyes.

The light changed. Nikki headed toward the vehicle to get a closer look. She verified the personal license plates—WINMD. A slow smile came across her face. She glanced over at Corina, who appeared confused as to what was going on in her head.

"What are you thinking?" Corina inquired.

"Do you still have that baseball bat in your truck?"

Corina tilted her head to one side. "What? Why?"

Nikki arched an eyebrow. She was still wobbly in the knees. "Just answer the question. Do you still have the bat, yes or no?"

"What are you going to do?" Corina threw her hands up in a surrendering gesture. "Never mind. I don't want to know."

"This has nothing to do with you." Nikki took off toward Corina's truck. She stopped in the middle of the street. "Where did you park?" She closed her eyes a moment. "Oh yeah." She took off again until she reached the vehicle. Looking in the trailer bed, she removed the bat and headed back to Winston's car.

Nikki concentrated on the windshield. It cracked. She landed blow after blow until the glass shattered. Satisfied, she moved to the side mirrors. The hits were accurate; both fell on the street. With each hit, she was feeling better. She proceeded to work on the driver side window. He will have plenty of fresh air on the way home, she thought. She quickly moved over to the passenger window. She stepped back, looking at her handiwork. A moment later, she looked to see Winston running toward her. He was cursing like a sailor.

Nikki made a beeline toward the truck. She hopped in on the passenger side and slid down in the seat. She was proud of her actions. He'd gotten what he deserved.

Corina got in, looking at Nikki in disbelief. She shook her head.

"Did you see his face?" Nikki laughed. "He couldn't believe what was happening to him."

"Proud of yourself?" Corina asked. "I can't believe you just did that. You're a doctor, for heaven's sake."

Nikki sat up. She looked over at Corina. Her eyes were on the road. She was gripping the steering wheel. Her friend was angry. She had never seen her so upset.

Nikki sat up straight in the seat. "Corina, are you upset?"

Corina took a quick glance at Nikki. "What do you think? I can't believe you did that."

"He deserved it," Nikki replied.

"Maybe he did, but I'm surprised that you would stoop to his level," Corina said. "First you attack him in the club, and now you damage his car. I don't want to know how he will react."

Nikki ran a hand across her throbbing forehead. "I didn't think that far ahead," she admitted.

"That's right," Corina said. "You didn't think. He's probably on the phone right now with the police."

Nikki gasped. "The police?" She didn't want to go to jail. She'd never had a parking ticket.

"Yes, the police," Corina repeated. "We may be going to jail."

"What do you mean 'we'? You didn't do anything."

"I'm driving the getaway vehicle." Corina moved into the left lane, then out onto the interstate.

"Getaway vehicle," Nikki said. Hearing her friend's concern reminded her of the famous white Bronco scene. She heard police sirens and looked out the rearview mirror. Her heart dropped into her stomach. The vehicles zoomed passed them. She let out a sigh of relief.

Thirty minutes later, Corina parked in front of Nikki's apartment building. "Do you need me to walk up with you?"

She exited the truck and strolled around to the passenger side. Opening the door, she helped Nikki out of the vehicle.

Nikki's legs felt like rubber. If she could stand, she could walk. "No, I got it. I'll talk to you later."

"All right," Corina said. Without another word, she climbed back into the vehicle and drove off.

Nikki stood a moment; she watched until the red lights disappeared. Her best friend could be in trouble for something that she did. She could never let that happen.

Nikki turned and headed into the building. She slowly walked across the lobby to the elevator. The doors opened, she got on, and rode it to the 5th floor. She managed to find her way to her apartment. She leaned against the doorframe. Her head was pounding. Digging down in her bag, she found the key. It took her a few minutes, but she managed to unlock the door.

She walked into the bedroom. She did not bother to undress or remove her shoes. She fell across the bed and passed out.

* * *

"Oh, my head," Nikki groaned the next morning. It felt like a hammer was hitting her over the head. Her body was aching. She slowly sat up and fell back on the pillow. Staring up at the ceiling, she tried to focus, but even her eyes were hurting. She lay still to allow the room to stop spinning. What happened last night? She closed her eyes. Corina's face floated in and out. They were at Cadence, drinking, everything after that was fuzzy. "Oh God, what did I do?"

Nikki threw her legs off the bed. The movement felt like she'd been run over by a Mack truck. It'd been years since she had a hangover. The way she was feeling made her remember why she couldn't drink. She made it to her feet. Holding on to the wall, she stumbled down the hallway and into the kitchen to prepare a concoction to help sober her up. It was good that she was still on vacation. Working was out of the question. She whipped up honey sandwiches and a small glass of Bloody Mary.

Thirty minutes later, Nikki hopped into the shower. The cold water was relaxing, and just what she needed to wake up. She toweled herself dry and headed into her bedroom. She put lotion on every part of her body. Walking over to the dresser, Nikki removed underwear, a gray North Carolina sweatshirt, and black leggings. She combed her hair into a ponytail. She was ready for the day.

She was headed toward the living room when her cellular phone rang. It was from the hospital. She gulped. After getting herself together, she sat on the foot of the bed and answered the call. "Dr. Phillips," she managed to say.

"Good morning, Dr. Phillips, this is Dr. Anderson. How are you?"

"I'm much better now. I'm ready to come back to work." Dr. Nathan Anderson was head of the orthopedic clinic. If he was calling her, it must be a serious matter.

Dr. Anderson was silent a moment. "That's what I want to talk to you about. Can you come into my office this morning?"

Nikki heard him flipping through his calendar. Dr. Anderson was still old-school. Besides a phone, he didn't own anything electronic.

"What about ten o'clock?"

"I'll be there," Nikki answered. She ended the call and immediately contacted Corina.

"Maybe Dr. Anderson is going to ask you to return to work," Corina suggested. "You were thinking of returning this week anyway."

"He could have asked me that on the phone," Nikki said. "I think something else is going on."

"You think Winston told him about last night?"

Nikki frowned. "Last night? What are you talking about?"

"You don't remember getting drunk last night and busting out the windows in Winston's Mercedes?"

Nikki closed her eyes and images of her swinging the bat and laughing appeared in her mind. She replayed running into Winston, the fight, and her smashing the windows in his vehicle. She was embarrassed. She couldn't believe she'd reacted that way. She was an educated, professional, and independent woman. Winston wasn't the last man on earth. Emotionally she was hurting, but her mother had taught her that time healed all wounds. In time, she would get over him.

"Corina, I'm so sorry, I can't believe that I did that."

"You were hurting. Upset," Corina said. "You had to get it out. You took it out on him and then his car."

"That's no excuse," Nikki said. "I'm a bigger woman than that. What if Winston presses charges?"

"The man is a jerk, but he wouldn't do that."

"Wouldn't he? I made a fool of him and myself."

"Maybe you can talk to Winston. Try and smooth things over," Corina suggested. "Or agree to pay for the damages. He might go for it and not press charges. I mean, it's not like he's innocent in this whole thing."

"I'm sure Winston doesn't see it that way," Nikki said. "He loved that car. He restored it. At times, I believed he loved it more than me." She chuckled. "I was right."

"Then what are you going to do?" Corina asked. "I'm too cute to go to jail."

"No one is going to jail," Nikki assured her. "I'll just go see what is going on. Then I'll talk with Winston and offer to pay for the damages."

"Good luck."

"I'll call you later."

* * *

As soon as Nikki strolled into the orthopedic clinic, staff members began whispering to each other. She held her head high and headed straight to Dr. Anderson's office. She knocked on the door.

"Come in," Dr. Anderson said.

Nikki walked into the office to find Dr. Anderson and a beautiful, elegantly dressed woman sitting next to Winston. She recognized Aliessa Coffer. She stopped in mid-step. She wasn't sure what the other woman was doing here, and she didn't have a good feeling about the meeting.

"Come on in, Dr. Phillips," Dr. Anderson said. He sat behind the desk, his hands clasped together on top of a stack of manila folders. "I'm glad you could make it on such a short notice. Have a seat."

Nikki nervously dropped down in a brown chair next to Winston. She watched as Aliessa leaned over and whispered something in Winston's ear. He bobbed his head up and down.

Nikki was the first to speak. "Dr. Anderson, your call sounded urgent. What did you want to talk to me about?"

Dr. Anderson cleared his throat. "I'm glad you came. This situation is urgent."

"You bet it is," Winston threw in.

Nikki had been with Winston long enough to know when he was upset. He was boiling mad about what had happened last night. She refocused on Dr. Anderson. "What's going on, Dr. Anderson?"

"You know I am a straightforward kind of guy," Dr. Anderson began. "I'm not going to beat around the bush here."

Nikki sat up straight.

"You never should have put your hands on me," Winston threw out.

Dr. Anderson glared at Winston. "Dr. Thorpe, please, let me handle this."

"Then handle it," Winston said. He glared at Nikki.

Nikki looked at her ex-fiancé in disbelief. He was so proud of himself. He seemed to take pleasure in what was going on.

"Nikki, what happened last night between you and Dr. Thorpe?" Dr. Anderson asked.

"I don't know," Nikki answered.

Winston stood. "What do you mean, you don't know?" He repeated in disbelief. "You attacked me. Busted out all of the windows in my Mercedes with a bat."

"What about what you did to me?" Nikki threw back at him. "You used me. Led me on for five years, and then you dumped me. Next thing I know you're getting married." She pointed a finger in his face. "You're lucky I didn't use that bat on you."

Winston leaned back. His voice rose an octave. "See that, Dr. Anderson? The woman is crazy."

"Oh yeah, I'm crazy for ever getting involved with a low down, dirty bastard like you."

"All right, that's enough, you two," Dr. Anderson yelled. "Both of you go to your neutral corners." He refocused on Nikki. "Did you attack him and break out all of the windows in his car?"

"I was drunk. I don't remember everything that happened last night."

"I have witnesses who saw you running away with bat in hand," Winston yelled.

She felt like she wanted to die. The meeting wasn't going well. Dr. Anderson rubbed his forehead, then said, "Dr. Phillips, you know the board frowns on this type of behavior, especially from employees in your position. You're a doctor. A good one, too. A role model. It's your job to set an example for the others."

Nikki knew the reputation of the board of directors very well. The board consisted of a bunch of good old boys who gave generous donations to the hospital. They didn't know the first thing about medicine but had enough money to buy a seat. She realized that the situation didn't look good, but it was her first and only black mark. She should be able to get off with a warning.

"I know," Nikki said in a desperate tone. She looked over at Winston. "I'm sorry, Winston. I apologize. I will pay to have your car repaired. I admit I lost my head. It will never happen again."

"You're right, it won't," Winston answered.

Nikki tilted her head to one side. She focused on Dr. Anderson. He dropped his gaze. The atmosphere turned cold. Serious. She stood. "What is this? You're firing me? What did I do to get fired?"

"I'm sorry, Dr. Phillips. You are one of our best and brightest, but what you did is against what this hospital stands for. We have to set an example. We can't have our doctors behaving in this manner. It looks bad for the hospital."

"Especially if the father-in-law is on the board of directors," Nikki threw back.

Dr. Anderson cleared his throat. Winston didn't answer.

"That's right," Aliessa said with satisfaction.

"I worked my butt off to get where I am, and now you're going to take that away from me to get me out of the way," Nikki replied.

"You should have thought about that before you did what you did," Winston snapped.

Nikki fought back the tears. This is unfair, she thought. She had lost everything that mattered to her. Her career. Her man. Her pride.

"Dr. Anderson, you said it yourself. I am an excellent surgeon. I know I lacked judgment on what I did; try to look at it from my point of view. This hospital needs me."

Dr. Anderson let out a deep sigh. "I understand."

"I don't. Begging won't help." Winston focused on Dr. Anderson. "You're not taking her side."

"No. He's not," Aliessa said in a warning tone.

"I'm not begging." Nikki said.

"I'm not taking anyone's side," Dr. Anderson replied. "I only said that I understand." He gave Winston a hard glance. "And I do."

"Dr. Anderson, you are just here to do your job, not sympathize," Winston said in a threatening voice. "So, do your job."

Nikki looked from one doctor to another. The situation was clear—Winston had talked to his father-in-law to be and had her fired. She didn't stand a chance. She stared at Winston. She didn't recognize the man standing in front of her. Where was all of the hate coming from? He of all people knew how much she loved being an orthopedic surgeon and what she'd done to make it happen.

Dr. Anderson paused a moment to collect his thoughts. "I'm sorry, Dr. Phillips. The board held an emergency meeting this morning. They decided that your services are no longer needed."

Nikki didn't wait to hear the rest. She turned and rushed out of the room. The tears began to fall.

* * *

An hour later, Nikki hurried into her apartment. She made a beeline to the bedroom. She entered the walk-in closet and removed a large suitcase from the top shelf. Corina was right; it was time for a vacation. She needed a nice, long trip.

She started putting clothing and shoes in the suitcase. Moving over to the dresser, she opened the top drawer and pulled out undergarments.

Deep sobs racked her inside, and she sat on the edge of the bed and cried uncontrollably.

A few minutes later, Nikki brushed away the tears as she made her way into the bathroom to gather toiletries. On the way back to the bedroom, she grabbed her overnight case and threw everything into it.

She grabbed her purse off the dresser and hiked it over her shoulder. Clutching the handle on the luggage, she rolled it through the living room and out the door.

Nikki arrived at the car, opened the car door, and tossed the suitcase on the backseat. She settled behind the wheel, then backed out of the parking space. She did not have a destination in mind. She stopped at the traffic light when it came to her. Home. It was time to head to Montgomery, Texas.

* * *

"I'll see you at the party later on, right?" Blake said to Ross. He nuzzled the neck of the busty brunette clinging to him. She giggled.

"I'll be there later." Ross was sitting at the dining room table. He never looked up from the novel he was reading, War and Peace.

"I see someone is getting the party started early." Junior laughed, coming in the front door. "Does she have a friend?

"Matter of fact, she does have a friend," Blake said then thrust his tongue down her throat.

"Is she pretty?" Junior asked.

"I don't have ugly friends," the woman said.

"My apologies, ma'am. I didn't mean no disrespect," Junior answered. "It's just that I prefer not to go to the party alone. If you have a friend, maybe you can call and invite her over."

The woman grinned. "I can do that." She reached in the front pocket of the Western-style blue shirt she was wearing. "What about you, Ross? Do you need a date for the party? I have another girlfriend that would be perfect for you."

"No, thank you." Ross never looked up from the book. He flipped the page.

"Ross doesn't date," Junior blurted out.

"He doesn't date," the woman teased.

Ross didn't flinch. He was still deep in the book.

"He's still nursing a broken heart," Junior said.

"TMI," Ross said in a calm tone, his eyes still glued to the book.

The brother's laughter filled the room.

"TMI?" The woman asked.

"Too much information," Blake explained.

Junior chuckled. "All the calves have been vaccinated. But two of the tractors stopped working. They just quit on us."

"Call Dan Whittier in the morning," Ross answered. "Have him come and take a look."

"Already done," Junior replied. "Ross, did Doc Baker say anything to you about him retiring?"

Ross's head finally snapped up. "Dr. Baker retiring? When?"

"Soon as he can get out of here is what he told me."

"Is he old enough to retire?" Blake asked. "What is he, sixty? Maybe he isn't retiring, but just leaving RFK. He's fed up with the rodeo life.

55

The traveling, injuries, and the deaths. He's not a young man anymore. It does take a toll on you after awhile."

"I can't see Dr. Baker leaving." Junior said. "If he does who's going to replace him. It won't be easy to replace the head of the Gallop Clinic."

"He's on the board of directors." Ross said. "Could be he's just leaving the clinic. I see what I can find out."

"I'm sorry, Junior." Blake's date interrupted their conversation. "My girlfriend has other plans for the evening, but says if she can get away she will join us later."

"Maybe it's best to go stag," Junior said. "That way I can mingle with all of the young ladies."

"It's Mr. Spaulding's sixty-fifth birthday party," Ross pointed out. "I don't think too many young ladies will be there."

Junior scratched his head in confusion. "The sooner we leave for the party. The sooner, I can leave and head over to The Big Boot."

"I'm sure you'll enjoy The Big Boot. You'll be able to line dance, play pool, and fall off the mechanical bull," Ross teased.

"And don't forget the drinks." Junior laughed. "It's the only nightspot in fifty miles that serves good liquor. I plan to get good and drunk. Hopefully not leave alone."

Ross only shook his head and said. "That's the last thing you need to do. You know you can't hold your liquor. I'm not bailing you out of jail."

"You know he likes to tear up the place," Blake teased.

"You should talk," Ross said.

"No one asked you too bail me out." Junior said.

"Good to know. I wasn't going too." Ross said. "If you get in trouble tonight, you will wake up in jail."

"I've been there before. Can I ride with you over to the Spaulding's?" Junior asked, changing the subject.

"Sure." Ross stood. "What about Dad?"

"He already went over," Blake replied.

"Let's get going," Junior said.

✳ ✳ ✳

Nikki turned the radio dial, searching for a music station to keep her company. All she had been able to pick up was static. On the road for over twenty hours, she was tired, hungry, and sleepy. Her legs were cramped from sitting so long. She looked out the car window. The sign read: Houston 110 miles. She noticed a tower and decided to scan for a station. She locked in on 90.1 WNOL FM. The song "Love Will Keep Us Together," by Captain and Tennille filled the car. She began singing and tapping a staccato on the steering wheel to stay awake.

She didn't want to admit it, but she was looking forward to seeing her family. Maybe this would be a good opportunity to try and work things out with her mother. Anxious to get home, she decided to exit Interstate 10 and pick up Route 85. It ran through the small town of Norstrom. It could cut off several hours of travel time. She stomped down on the gas.

She skillfully shifted the BMW around a sharp curve. The bags on the front seat slid to the floor. Food spilled everywhere.

She grabbed a napkin and leaned down, attempting to clean up the mess while keeping an eye on the road.

Nikki glanced away for just a second. The next thing she knew, she looked up to see several cows standing in the middle of the road. She swerved to avoid hitting the animals and lost control of the vehicle. The car skidded across the road and hit a barbwire fence. The impact uprooted several wooden poles from the ground, along with the rose shaped mailbox next to it.

When the vehicle came to a stop, the airbag ejected, hitting her in the face. She was so startled and scared that she couldn't move. Adrenaline was pumping throughout her body, and her trembling hands gripped the steering wheel.

She closed her eyes and laid her head back. For the next few minutes, she sat there, trying to shake loose the cobwebs.

"Are you alright, ma'am?" Nikki heard a voice asking through the fog. She slowly looked over and up into the face of two men surrounding the car.

"Ma'am, can you hear me?" the taller one asked. "Can you move?" He reached through the window and opened the door.

"Should we move her?" the shorter one said.

Nikki began to gingerly move. The taller one reached down, unsnapped the seat belt, and scooped her up in his strong arms. He carefully laid her on the grass a few feet away from the car. "Junior call 911," he commanded in a deep voice.

Maybe she'd been hit too hard, but she was turned on by the rescue. A long finger removed the hair from her face.

Nikki tried to sit up. "I'm fine. There's no need to call 911."

"Whoa now," the taller one said. He held a strong hand to her lower back. "You were just in a nasty accident. Take it easy. You need to get checked out. Junior called 911."

"I said there's no reason to call 911. I am all right," Nikki repeated. "I'm just a little dizzy."

"Maybe, ma'am," he said. "But I would feel a lot better if you were checked out. If you don't want us to call an ambulance, we have a clinic here at the ranch, and a doctor on staff. He could give you a quick examination."

When Nikki was able to focus, she saw her car resting on a mound of dirt. It was tangled in barbwire and twisted metal. She noticed a group of men on horseback leading cattle through the opening in the fence. Then she remembered what happened. The cows standing in the middle of the road.

Nikki turned toward the tall man. "This is your fault," she hissed. She slowly stood to her feet.

"Excuse me, ma'am?" He replied.

"You heard me. This is all your fault," Nikki repeated. She was frustrated and irritated. She could have lost her life. Her sad life flashed before her eyes. "If your cows weren't in the middle of the road, I wouldn't have crashed."

The man pushed the Stetson back on his head. "Cows?"

Looking at the tall drink of water standing before her caused a surge of heat to race through her body. He could quench any woman's thirst. But he was a man, and at the moment, she'd sworn off men.

"Ma'am, I apologize for the 'cattle,'" he corrected, "being in the road. They managed to get out. They do that sometimes. But RFK Ranch will pay for any car damages. Just have your insurance company contact us. If you decide later to get checked out by a doctor, send us the bill." He pulled out his wallet, removed a business card, and handed it to Nikki.

Nikki looked at the name on the card—Ross Kincaid. She then looked at him with attitude. She spread her arms apart and said. "Mr. Kincaid? That's it? That's all you have to say?"

Ross frowned. He looked at her like she'd lost her mind. He didn't understand why she was behaving the way she was. He'd admitted fault. They'd agreed to pay for any and all damages. What was there left to say? He figured she was all right because she was up in arms.

She placed her hands on top of her head and walked around, checking the damage to the vehicle. "Look at my car."

"Ma'am," Ross tried to interject.

"Please stop calling me ma'am. It's annoying," she screamed.

Ross leaned back. "I'm sorry. Most women appreciate the term of address."

"I'm not most women."

"I can see that," Ross said in a calm tone.

"It makes me feel like an old woman."

"And you definitely ain't that," the shorter one chimed in. He openly looked her up and down.

Nikki rolled her eyes in aggravation.

"Franklin Kincaid, Junior." He smiled and stuck out a hand. "You can call me Junior. It's a pleasure to meet you."

Nikki looked at his hand a moment before extending her. "Nicole Phillips."

Junior smiled. "Nicole Phillips. Cute name. Can we call you a tow?"

"I have AAA," Nikki boasted.

"They will take forever to get here," Junior replied. He whipped out his cell phone. "I will call someone I know. They will be here in no time."

Nikki ran a hand across her forehead. She had a slight headache, and there was a small lump on the back of her head.

"Are you sure you don't want to get looked at?" Ross asked. "You could have a concussion."

"I said I'm all right. It's nothing Tylenol and rest can't fix," Nikki replied.

"You seem to be more concerned with the car than your health," Ross replied.

Nikki placed both hands on her hips. She didn't know what it was about this man that got under her skin. Everything he said and did rubbed her the wrong way. "Whose fault is it that I lost control of my car?"

"Ma'am," Ross answered in a sarcastic tone.

"Nicole," Nikki snapped back. "I believe I said my name is Nicole Phillips. It is not ma'am. Folks call me, Nikki."

"Fine, Nikki," Ross said in a condescending tone, "if you were not speeding you would have been able to stop in time."

Her eyes stretched. "What? I wasn't speeding."

"Yes. You were," Ross quipped. "I noticed your car coming around the curve, and you were traveling pretty fast. There is a sign posted warning drivers of livestock crossing and a reduction in speed."

Nikki drew her eyebrows together. She didn't remember seeing a sign about livestock crossing or a decrease in speed. "There wasn't any sign about livestock or reducing speed."

"It could have been knocked down again," Junior said.

"Again?" Nikki repeated.

"Yeah, some of the young folks around here like to pull pranks," Junior explained. "It's their idea of having fun."

"Someone needs to have a little chat with them," Nikki replied. "It's dangerous."

"If that's what happened," Ross continued. He walked over and grabbed the horse by the reins.

Chapter Four

"There was no sign," Nikki exclaimed to the Sheriff thirty-minutes later.

"High school prank." Sheriff Cabot removed his hat and ran his short, stubby fingers through his graying hair. "I have to have a talk with them youngsters." He was a short, stocky man with a pudgy face and belly to match.

He' been in office for the past twenty years. He knew everyone in Norstrom. The citizens admired and trusted him.

Nikki noticed a large wad of tobacco in his right jaw. She couldn't believe people still indulged in such a filthy habit. He spat on the ground. She frowned and looked away. Disgusting.

"You know who did it, Sheriff?" Junior inquired.

"Oh, I have a pretty good idea," Sheriff Cabot replied. "I'll be talking to some parents."

"Ma'am, I'll be taking your car in now," the tow truck driver relayed as he raised her vehicle onto the back of the trailer. He walked over and handed Nikki a slip of paper. "It will be at this address."

"How long do you think it will take to repair it?" Nikki asked.

"From what I can see right now, the front axle is broken," the man answered. "Won't know what else is wrong until it's on the rack."

"So, you can't tell me how long it's going to take," Nikki replied in a stern tone.

The man looked at her in surprise. "Where are you coming from, ma'am?"

Nikki glanced around at the faces of the four men gawking at her. She was the center of attention. At the moment, she felt like she was under a microscope. "I'm from Washington, D.C. Why?"

Ross chuckled. He dipped his head. "That explains a lot."

She swirled around to face him. "What is that supposed to mean?"

"It means there is no reason to be rude to Jake," Ross said. "He didn't have to leave his comfortable bed to take care of your vehicle. You should show some respect."

Nikki didn't miss the grin on Jake's face. "Isn't that Jake's job?" she snapped.

Jake's smile slipped.

Ross released a deep sigh. "No, it isn't. Jake is the deputy sheriff. The owner of Mack's Towing Service is out of town. As a favor to us, he volunteered to come and tow you on his day off."

Nikki swallowed the lump in her throat. It wasn't Jake's fault. She was mad at the situation. Nothing was working out, not even her escape. She was stranded in a backwater town being belittled by a wannabe cowboy. How could the situation get worse?

"Say thank you," Ross instructed.

"What?" Nikki replied in disbelief. "Why should I?"

Ross boldly walked over and stood in front of her. His six- foot frame was intimidating. There was chemistry between them. Bad chemistry. "Because around these parts, there is such a thing as manners."

Nikki folded her arms across her chest. "Well, it's a good thing I am not from around these parts," she imitated in a thick Texas drawl.

Ross smirked. "Enough of this, Sheriff Cabot." He pointed to Nikki. "I'd like to press charges against this woman."

She unfolded her arms. "What? What for?"

"You did take out our fence," Ross reminded her.

"Yeah, but—" she tried to say.

"And our mailbox," Ross continued. "It's not cheap. It was a special order."

"Now look here—" Nikki tried to say again.

"I'd say we're looking at...at least a couple thousand dollars' worth of damage, just for the fence alone," Ross continued.

Nikki's mouth gaped. "I'm not paying one cent," she said. "This is robbery. It's not my fault the sign wasn't there."

"We don't know that, do we?" Ross replied. "The way I see it, ma'am, you're responsible for the damages."

"What's going on here?" A voice boomed from behind them. "I heard there was an accident. Someone is hurt."

Nikki turned to see a silver-haired middle-aged man casually moving toward them. He was walking with a cane.

"Nothing to concern yourself about, Doc Baker," Sheriff Cabot said. "This young lady was in an accident but refused medical treatment."

Dr. Baker drew his thick white eyebrows together. "How are you feeling, miss? Are you sure you don't want to be examined? We have a clinic on the ranch." He pointed with the cane. "It will only take a moment. You may have a concussion."

"I already said I'm fine. I wish everyone would stop asking me."

"Just showing concern, that's all," Dr. Baker said.

"This lady," Ross emphasized, "is from D.C. She doesn't know anything about good manners."

"I'm sure that ain't true," Dr. Baker replied.

"At this point, I don't care." Ross focused on Sheriff Cabot. "Sheriff, do your job. I want her arrested for personal property damage."

"Ross, be serious," Junior protested. "Aren't you taking this too far?"

Ross smirked. "Not at all. I don't think I've gone far enough. This lady needs to learn some manners."

Nikki couldn't believe what was happening. She was going to jail for something that wasn't her fault. Sheriff Cabot headed toward her. She took a step back.

"Come along, ma'am. There has been a complaint against you. I have to take you in." From his back, he withdrew a set of handcuffs.

"Sheriff, are those necessary?" Junior voiced in disbelief.

"It's protocol," Sheriff Cabot replied. He clicked them on her wrists.

"I don't think the young lady is a criminal," Dr. Baker said. "The handcuffs are not needed."

"Wait a second!" Nikki exclaimed. "I'm a doctor." She usually didn't drop the occupation card, but this was an emergency.

"Good for you, ma'am." Sheriff Cabot guided her by the elbow. He led her to the cruiser and placed her in the backseat.

Dr. Baker walked over and stuck his head in the back window. "What kind of doctor are you?" he asked.

"I'm an orthopedic surgeon at Bayside General Hospital in D.C.," Nikki pleaded. "You can verify it. My name is Dr. Nicole Phillips." She noticed Junior and Dr. Baker glanced at each other. Ross seemed unimpressed.

Dr. Baker leaned his head back through the window. "I'll make a phone call, Dr. Phillips. Don't worry," he said as the police cruiser drove off. "Was that necessary?" he asked Ross. He tapped the cane in the dirt. "You were the one without manners."

"Yes, it was necessary." Ross said. "She was rude and disrespectful. We all saw her terrible attitude. She needed to be taken down a notch."

"What about you?" Junior chimed. "You were just as disrespectful."

Ross didn't bother to answer. He refocused on Dr. Baker. "Doc, I hear you're thinking of retiring."

"I was having doubts about it," Dr. Baker said. "Now, I'm not so sure."

Without another word, Ross walked over and swung his long legs over Bullet. "We have to get going. I don't want to be late for the party." He nudged the horse and galloped toward the house. He thought that maybe he'd been a little overzealous in his actions. The way he saw it the good doctor needed someone to put her in her place. He was just the man to do it. She was looking down her nose at them.

He hadn't been fazed by a woman since Hailey. He couldn't believe he'd allowed her to get under his skin. It didn't matter; she would soon be on her way, and he would never have to see her again.

* * *

The party was in full swing when Ross arrived. Junior had declined to ride with him in protest of the handling of Nikki. It was all right with him; he was in no mood to hear him complain all the way over to the Spaulding's.

He looked to see that his brothers had already arrived. They both had dates. Watching the scene, he couldn't help but feel a twinge of jealousy. It'd been a while since he'd been on a date. It wasn't for a lack of willing females. On the rodeo circuit, there was a constant string of women throwing themselves at him. But he wanted more than just an occasional roll in the hay. He hoped to one day settle down with a loving and loyal wife and have a house full of children.

His mind thought of Nikki. He had to admit, she was smart, beautiful, and feisty. But she wasn't the type of woman he'd take to his bed. He pitied the man that she would marry. From what he'd just witnessed, she'd be a handful.

"It's about time you showed up," Lena cooed, throwing her arms around his neck. She kissed him on the cheek. "I was beginning to think that you weren't going to make it."

"I figured I would be in big trouble if I didn't come," Ross answered.

"You got that right." Lena locked her arm in his. "The important thing is that you are here now."

"What did I miss?" Ross asked.

"Me, of course," Lena replied.

Ross gulped. He wished he could share Lena's affection. He changed the subject. "Where's your father?"

Lena poked her bottom lip out. "You sure know how to hurt a girl," she pouted, pulling on his arm. "He's out back with your father and several of the other ranchers. Harper had to go out of town."

"Thanks," Ross said. "I'll go say hi. I'll talk to you later." He headed outside.

"Here he comes," Mr. Spaulding exclaimed as Ross strolled out into the spacious backyard. The music of a country band had the guests doing a line dance. A large *Happy 65th Birthday* banner hung between two large tree branches. A champagne fountain stood in the middle of the yard.

"Norstrom local rodeo champion," Mr. Spaulding exclaimed.

He waved Ross over. "Come on over here, boy."

Ross was embarrassed. He didn't like attention, but he could tell Mr. Spaulding was good and drunk. "Mr. Spaulding, how have you been?"

"These old bones got me up this morning," Mr. Spaulding answered. "That's saying something."

"You mean old coot; you are too stubborn to die," Franklin Sr. said.

Everyone burst out laughing.

"I'll overlook that, since it's you, you old fart," Spaulding replied. He refocused on Ross. "Congratulations on winning the Southern Invitational. Will you be competing in the Sweet Bronco Invitational in Houston? The purse is fifteen thousand."

Ross looked at his father, who took a sip of champagne and then walked off. He dropped his eyes in disappointment.

"I see he is still against you riding," Mr. Spaulding pointed out. "He's just concerned about you, that's all. I don't have to tell you about the consequences. You see what happened to my Harper."

"Yeah, well, he never got over my last nasty spill."

"I admit, I didn't think you would have the nerve to ride again, or get back on the bull." Mr. Spaulding hiccupped. "But then, you are a Kincaid. Balls of steel, just like your old man. In his day, he was a damn good rider before he was forced to quit. Do what is best for you."

"I always do," Ross replied. He stayed at the party a few hours more before calling it a night.

* * *

The next morning, Nikki found herself on the way to the courthouse to be arraigned. She stepped out of the building into the fresh air. The sunshine on her face made her feel alive. It was needed after spending a night in a cold, dreary jail. She didn't get much sleep. The bed was hard, the pillow was flat, and the blanket was itchy. Though she was the only one in her cell, she didn't feel comfortable going to the bathroom. It was embarrassing. The Sheriff and his deputies were pleasant enough, waiting on her hand and foot. But it didn't make up for her being behind bars.

Ross Kincaid was a neanderthal; that was plain and simple. She was not going to forget the way he treated her. Her pride, heart, and reputation were being trampled on by another man. First, it was Winston and now Ross. Both were walking over her.

She was beginning to feel like a doormat. When was it going to end?

"The courthouse is next door," Sheriff Cabot explained. "We will get you arraigned and see if we can get you on your way."

"It sounds simple," Nikki replied. "What about bail?"

"I wouldn't worry about that, ma'am," Sheriff Cabot said. "Does this happen to everyone passing through Norstrom?" Nikki inquired.

Sheriff Cabot spat tobacco on the ground. "Little lady, that mouth of yours is what got you in this mess. I would be more careful if I were you."

"No, Ross Kincaid is what got me in this situation," she emphasized.

Sheriff Cabot stopped in his tracks. "Let me give you some good advice. This old boy was born and raised around these parts. The Kincaid's run this town. They have lots of money, power, and pull around here. So, I'd be careful if I were you."

"That sounds like a threat," Nikki replied.

"It's not a threat, just some sound, friendly advice and here's some more. When you go before the judge, listen, don't say nothing, and you will be on your way in no time."

"How can I be on my way?" Nikki argued. "My car was towed."

"Don't worry that pretty little head about that." Sheriff Cabot said. "I called the shop this morning to see about getting a rush on fixing your vehicle."

"Maybe I can rent a car?"

"Yes, there's a little private lot on the edge of town where you can get a vehicle," Sheriff Cabot said. "I can give you the details later, but I don't believe that will be necessary."

"Thanks, Sheriff," Nikki replied.

"No problem. We need to get going." Sheriff Cabot guided her by the elbow to the building next door. "Where are you from?"

"Montgomery," Nikki answered. "Born and raised."

Sheriff Cabot's face broke into a big smile. "You don't say. Lots of good folks in Montgomery. Who are your kin?"

"George and Sophie Phillips. My mother was a stay at home mom, and my dad runs a hardware store."

"Sounds like good folks," Sheriff Cabot replied. "Did you phone them? Let them know you were in trouble."

"How could I?" Nikki answered. "I was in a cell."

"You were entitled to one phone call, ma'am."

"I guess Jake didn't get the memo," Nikki said.

Sheriff Cabot smirked. "I'll have to talk to him about that."

Nikki didn't back down. "You should do that." She felt a small sense of satisfaction in telling Sheriff Cabot off, but he was right about one thing—she had to keep her emotions under control. Holding on to her temper has never been easy for her. But she wanted to get out of this town without another incident.

"Let's head on in," Sheriff Cabot instructed.

He opened the door. They walked down the small hallway. Nikki was grateful that the sheriff decided not to use the handcuffs. A moment later, he opened the door to courtroom one. She walked inside to find quite a few people already seated. She spotted Dr. Baker on the back row. Sitting next to him was a geeky-looking man in glasses. He looked to be in his late-twenties. Both men stood. She didn't miss the tight-fitting blue suit the young man was wearing.

"Good Morning, Dr. Phillips," Dr. Baker spoke. "Sheriff. It's good to see you both again."

"Morning, Dr. Baker," Nikki said. "What are you doing here so early in the morning?"

"Doc," Sheriff Cabot replied. "This little lady is about to be arraigned."

"That's why we're here. I want to introduce my nephew Andrew Dunsmore. He happens to be an excellent attorney," Dr. Baker explained.

"We spoke with Franklin Kincaid Sr. last night and talked him into making a deal for the court that I believe will work out for both parties."

"Deal?" Nikki asked as Andrew and Dr. Baker whisked her toward the front of the courtroom. "What kind of deal?" She took her position between the two men.

"Case number 71532 Kincaid vs. Phillips," the bailiff announced as he handed a brown folder to a middle-aged black man dressed in a black robe.

Nikki read Judge Ralph Spears on the nameplate. She tried to put on a strong face, but she was shaking like a leaf on a tree.

"Don't worry," Dr. Baker said. "Everything is going to be alright."

* * *

"Kincaid vs. Phillips," Ralph Spears said, opening the file. "Who's representing the prosecution?" he asked, putting on a pair of reading glasses.

"Attorney Jonathan Nickles here for the prosecution," a tall, dark haired young, Caucasian man said strolling into the courtroom. He appeared to be in his mid-thirties, wearing an expensive gray suit with matching shoes. Handsome. The man didn't have a hair out of place. He looked like he stepped out of the pages of *GQ Magazine*. Behind him, Ross was bringing up the rear. The two men together was sweet eye candy.

Nikki gulped. Why was he here? She looked him up and down. The tight black jeans he was wearing encased long, powerful thighs. All of the women's eyes in the court followed him to the front of the room. He should be the one on trial for looking that good. *Life isn't fair*, she said to herself.

"A deal was reached late last night in this case," Attorney Dunsmore explained. "Franklin Kincaid Sr. whose property was damaged and his son Ross Kincaid, who filed charges against the defendant." He reached into the black briefcase and removed several documents. He handed them to the bailiff, who gave them to Judge Spears.

Nikki was flabbergasted. She leaned over and whispered to Dr. Baker, "Why didn't someone tell me a deal was made? And what is Ross Kincaid doing here?"

"There wasn't time," Dr. Baker answered. "And Ross was the person filing charges against you. It's only natural he would be here."

"What do we have?" Judge Spears read aloud. "Property damage in the amount of twenty-five thousand dollars."

Nikki couldn't believe her ears. "What?" she yelled out. "That is ridiculous. There is no way I did that kind of damage. It's a fence!"

Judge Spears banged the gavel on the bench. "Quiet!"

Nikki was startled. She almost jumped out of her skin.

"Speak when you are spoken to." Judge Spears focused on Attorney Dunsmore. "Mr. Dunsmore control your client."

"Dr. Phillips, please," Dr. Baker scolded. "Judge Spears looks like a good ole, sweet man, but trust me, he isn't. Rub him the wrong way, and you will have a bad day."

Nikki looked over and spotted Sheriff Cabot sitting behind Ross and Attorney Nickels. He nodded.

"Your Honor, may I address the court?" Attorney Dunsmore asked.

"You may." Judge Spears said.

"As I mentioned earlier, a deal was proposed by the RFK Ranch about paying for the property damages caused by Miss Phillips," Attorney Dunsmore said. "You have a copy of the agreement there in front of you."

"What is the proposal?" Judge Spears inquired, scanning the document.

"Your Honor, Miss Phillips was an orthopedic surgeon at Bayside General Hospital in Washington, D.C."

"What do you mean was?" Judge Spears leaned back in the chair. He looked over his glasses at Nikki.

"Well, she was let go a couple of days ago because of a personal matter, not professional," Attorney Dunsmore explained.

"Oh my God," Nikki said aloud. "Did you have to mention that?" She wanted to find a hole and crawl in it. Everyone was looking at her and whispering. Ross shook his head.

"What's your point, Mr. Dunsmore?"

"The point is that Franklin Kincaid Sr. has proposed that Dr. Phillips work at the Gallop Clinic at RFK Ranch to pay for the damages."

Nikki's mouth gaped. "What? No way. Your Honor, why can't I just pay for the damages? she explained. "I'm on my way to Montgomery to visit my family. I haven't see my parents in over five years. I really would like to see them."

Judge Spears waited for her to finish her explanation. "Are you done?"

Nikki dropped her gaze. She was embarrassed. "Yes, Your Honor."

"Good. You might want to tell them that you will be a little late." Judge Spears continued reading the document. "About two-weeks late. From what I'm reading, the Kincaid's seem to think that it will be too easy for the defendant to pay the damages and be on her way. A lesson has to be learned about responsibility."

Nikki held her tongue. There was so much she wanted to say but didn't dare.

"I agree with them. You're an orthopedic surgeon. The Gallop Clinic can use your experience for the next couple of weeks," Judge Spears explained. "Many of the local boys will be competing in the Sweet Bronco Invitational. An extra pair of hands can come in handy."

"Judge Spears, can I say something?" Nikki was fuming. There was no way she wanted to be in the same vicinity as Ross Kincaid, and she has no interest in working in the Gallop Clinic.

"Your Honor, before Dr. Phillips objects to working at the Gallop Clinic," Mr. Nickles began, "she should know that if she doesn't accept the deal that she is looking at a minimum of six months in jail."

Nikki glared at Ross. He looked proud of himself. She wanted to knock the smirk off his face. He just delivered the knockout punch.

Judge Spears focused on her. "Dr. Phillips I am sentencing you to work at the Gallop Clinic for a total of at least two weeks. That should be enough time to pay for the damages." He looked at Ross. "Mr. Kincaid make sure that someone is keeping track of the defendant hours. She's not to work over the amount that is owed. Do you understand?"

"I understand, Your Honor." Ross answered.

Nikki shook her head in disbelief. It wasn't a dream, but a nightmare.

Ten minutes later, Nikki walked out of the courtroom on wobbly legs.

Attorney Dunsmore guided her by the elbow through the doors. "I do think this is the best decision for you."

"What are you talking about?" Nikki asked. "I was just blindsided in there. You and Dr. Baker should have discussed it with me before you agreed to this. There is no way I'm going to work for the people who put me in this situation. I won't do it." She pouted.

"You will do it," Ross said, coming up behind her. "If you don't, we can go back in the courtroom and tell Judge Spears that you changed your mind and would like six months jail time instead."

Nikki held her tongue. Ross Kincaid wasn't going to break her.

"Well? What's it going to be?" Ross prompted.

*   *   *

"Who's going to be working at the clinic?" Junior inquired as he scattered hay in the stalls.

"Dr. Phillips is going to be working at The Gallop Clinic to pay for the damages to the fence," Ross explained. "Dad and Dr. Baker came up with a pretty good argument to convince me that we could use another doctor for the next couple of weeks, especially with the Sweet Bronco Invitational coming up."

"Hey, you get no argument from me," Junior said. "She's a beauty, isn't she?"

Ross removed his work gloves. "I didn't notice," he lied.

"Any hot-blooded man can see that she's a beautiful woman, even you," Junior said.

"Can we just work please?" Ross asked.

"You like her," Junior teased.

Ross stopped in mid-motion. "Don't be ridiculous. She's not my type. Too feisty. I like my women more submissive."

Junior grinned. "I like them feisty. Keeps me on my toes. This one is a triple threat; she's beautiful, intelligent, and independent. The total package."

"For some city guy, those traits would be welcomed," Ross said. "This is rodeo country, we prefer women to be a lil' more submissive. You should know that since that is the only kind you date."

"At least I date," Junior replied. "When was the last time you had a date?"

"Is that what you call it?" Ross answered.

"Dr. Phillips could be the one."

Ross did his best not to laugh. "She's not your type," he said, tossing a bale of hay on the back of the flat-bed truck.

"Big brother, I'm every woman's type," Junior boasted. "I'm tall, dark, handsome, and rich. Those are all the qualities women are looking for."

"Yes, well, from what I can tell about the good doctor," Ross said, "that ain't what she's looking for."

"What else could it be?"

"I'm not sure what she's looking for," Ross replied.

"Whatever it is," Junior chuckled, "I'm more than happy to help her find it."

Ross shook his head. Junior was full of himself. He believed he was the answer to every woman's dream. But there was something about Dr. Nicole Phillips that told him she was looking for something much more than what his brother had to offer.

"Casanova, do you think you can muck out the stalls?"

"Afternoon, fellas," Dr. Baker spoke, strolling up behind them.

"Doc," the two men spoke in unison.

"Doc, I hear Dr. Phillips is going to be working at the clinic," Junior replied.

"Yes. For the next couple of weeks, thanks to your father and brother," Doctor Baker explained.

"Speaking of the clinic, Doc, have you thought about who's going to be your replacement?" Ross asked.

"I have a few people in mind," Dr. Baker replied.

"I hope it will be someone from the clinic." Ross said.

"Maybe," Doc Baker answered in a suspicious tone. "Maybe not."

"What brings you here?" Junior inquired.

"I wanted to let you know, Dr. Phillips will start at the clinic in the morning." Dr. Baker said.

"I'll be glad to show her around the clinic." Junior volunteer.

"No, you don't," Ross said. "Doc. Baker can do that."

"What about a place to stay?" Junior asked.

"She has family in Montgomery," Dr. Baker replied. "But the commute is too far. I'm hoping to get her a room at Mabelle's."

"That dump," Junior exclaimed. "It ain't no bigger than a rabbit hole."

"But it's neat and clean," Dr. Baker replied. "The food is good. She will be okay."

"Where do you suggest she stay?" Ross asked

"She can stay right here at RFK Ranch," Junior said.

Ross's eyes stretched. "Have you lost your mind? There's no way she can stay with us."

"Why not?" Junior asked. "We have plenty of room."

Ross noticed a look between his brother and Dr. Baker. "I see what's going on. It's two against one." He removed the cowboy hat and rubbed a hand over his head. "I'm not falling for it."

"No one is gaining up on you," Junior said. "Don't you feel sorry for her? The lady needs a roof over her head. If it weren't for you, she wouldn't be in this situation."

Ross let out a deep sigh. He wasn't going to let Junior or Dr. Baker put him in an uncomfortable position. "I know you are interested in the lady, but it ain't about to happen. She will be just fine at Mabelle's," he said. "Now, can we get back to work?"

* * *

"I don't understand why the Judge didn't allow me to pay for the damages and let me be on my way," Nikki said. She folded her arms across her chest and began pacing the floor in Mabelle's.

"You heard the judge," Dr. Baker said. "It's not about the money; they know you can pay. The Kincaid's want to teach you a lesson. Ross believes you disrespected him. It's his way of getting even."

Ross Kincaid. Whenever Nikki heard his name she wanted to scream. "You need me to work in your clinic?" she said.

"Dr. Phillips, we don't need you to work in the clinic. We have some of the finest doctors at the Gallop Clinic," Dr. Baker said. "I was helping out a fellow physician."

"Then help me out by talking to Judge Spears."

"So, you want to tuck your tail between your legs and run?" Dr. Baker replied. "I thought you were bigger than that. I guess I was wrong."

Nikki looked at Dr. Baker in surprise. "I can't believe you are using the guilt trip against me."

"I will if it gets you to grow a spine," Dr. Baker replied. "You are letting Ross Kincaid get to you. Look at you; you're all wound up and ready to pop."

Dr. Baker was right. Ross had gotten to her. She allowed him to get under her skin. "What should I do?"

"For one, get your thoughts together," Dr. Baker suggested. "It's not the end of the world. You were in an accident; it could have been worse, but you walked away. Be thankful for that. Second, stop lashing out at everyone. You're going around acting like everyone is against you. Some of us are just trying to help you, not harm you."

Nikki smiled at the analogy. What Dr. Baker said hit home.

"I don't know what or who you were running from in D.C.," Dr. Baker continued. "But I'm guessing it has something to do with you being let go from the hospital."

She sat in the chair. "That's personal."

Dr. Baker took the other chair across from her. "I'm not asking you to talk about what happened. When or if you want to talk, I am here. In the meantime, get that chip off your shoulder, work your hours, and be on your way."

"Ross Kincaid doesn't work in the clinic, does he?"

Dr. Baker chuckled. "No, he doesn't. I'm the boss at the clinic. Ross isn't a bad guy. He may have gone a little too far, but that was the Kincaid pride at work. They have a lot of that; get used to it."

"A little bit," Nikki said. "But you were right; I guess I have been acting like a 'B'."

"You said it." Dr. Baker chuckled. "Not me. Don't worry about Ross; he will get over it."

"Glad to hear it." Nikki took a deep breath. "Don't I need privileges to work in the clinic?"

"You're not on staff," Dr. Baker explained. "You will be working under me." He stood. "Just helping out."

"I figured that was the case," Nikki replied. "I will see you in the morning." She came to her feet and headed toward the door. "I don't know anything about the rodeo."

"All we need is your medical expertise," Dr. Baker said, stopping in front of the door. "A broken bone is just a broken bone."

It wasn't that Nikki couldn't handle the work. She needed a change of pace to take her mind off what was going on in her life, and it was only for a couple of weeks. She could do it, standing on her head.

* * *

"Mom, I was on my way home when the accident happened," Nikki said into the phone. "I'm okay. I was not hurt."

"I'm glad that you remember that you still have a family," Sophie threw in. "But at least you weren't hurt; that is most important."

Nikki closed her eyes a moment. "I just called to let you know that I am okay. I'll be home soon."

"Can you take that much time off?"

"I'm on sort of a leave of absence," Nikki lied. If she told her mother that she was let go, she'd never hear the end of it.

"What happened?" Sophie asked.

"It's nothing," Nikki said. "Besides, I will be working, not at a hospital but with the rodeo."

"The rodeo?" her mother said. "What on earth do you know about the rodeo?

"I don't know anything about it, but the judge ordered me to do Community Service to pay for the damages."

"The judge wouldn't allow you to pay your way out of it?" Sophie asked.

"No," Nikki answered. "I already asked."

"You're going to be fine," Sophie answered. "Time will fly by, and you will be home before you know it."

Nikki chatted with her mother a few minutes more before ending the call. She gathered her purse and hurried downstairs. The smell of bacon tingled her nose. As she landed on the last step, she noticed a sign that read: *Free Breakfast until 11 a.m.*

A few minutes later, she sat in a booth by the window with a plate of waffles, eggs, bacon, and a cup of coffee. She was famished. She looked out to see a light rain had begun to fall. People were leisurely moving in and out of shops. The town of Norstrom was the opposite of D.C. where citizens were rushing to and fro. They were always in a hurry, looking professional and political. She could never get use to this town. She might die from the boredom. She took a sip of coffee. It was awful. It tasted as if it had been filtered through a cowboy's pocket. What was she going to do without Starbucks? She may have been born in a small town, but she was a city girl at heart.

"Can I get you anything else, sugar?" The heavyset, middle-aged, dark hair woman, with too much makeup asked. She was chewing gum a mile a minute.

"No. Thank you."

"If you need anything just give a holla," she said in a thick, southern drawl.

Nikki looked to read the name on her nametag. "Thank you, Mabelle."

Mabelle smiled. "You ain't from around here, are you, sweetie?"

"No. I'm from D.C.," Nikki answered.

Mabelle arched an eyebrow. The young man in the booth in front of her turned around. He whispered something to the man across from him.

"You're the one that Doc Baker asked me to look after. You're a long way from home," Mabelle said.

"I agree." Nikki said.

"Folks call me, Mabelle." She extended a hand. "I run this place. What are you doing in Norstrom?"

"Nice to meet you, Mabelle," Nikki accepted her hand. "I'm going to be helping out at the Gallop Clinic for a couple of weeks."

"You're a doctor, right?"

"Yes," Nikki answered.

"Well, don't that beat all." Mabelle smiled. "You look too young to be a doctor. You're a pretty lil thing."

Nikki returned her smile. "Thank you."

"Welcome to Norstrom," Mabelle said. "We are a small and peaceful town. I was born and raised here. We ain't no D.C., but we hold our own. People can leave their doors unlocked, and folks are friendly."

"I can see that," Nikki said. "Different than where I'm coming from."

"We have good food, music, and some of the best rodeo riders in the country have come from Norstrom," Mabelle continued. "Rodeo is important to this town."

"Like football to the NFL," the young man passing by chimed in.

"That's right." Mabelle chuckled. "This is the home of the Rodeo Champion for the past three years."

"Who is the Champion?" Nikki asked out of curiosity.

"Ross Kincaid," Mabelle replied. "Who else?"

"Ross Kincaid?" Nikki repeated in disbelief. *That jerk was a Rodeo Champion*, she said to herself. That explains his macho attitude.

"The one and only," Mabelle answered.

Chapter Five

The next morning, Dr. Baker pulled in front of the Boarding House and honked the horn. Nikki hopped into the passenger seat, and they headed out of town. She phoned the mechanic to check on her vehicle. It would not be ready until the end of the week. A part had to be ordered. She glanced out the passenger window as they drove through the beautiful and wide countryside. She did not want to admit it, but Norstrom was breathtaking. The rich green pastures and farmers plowing the land was a sight to see. It brought back memories of growing up in Montgomery. They passed several ranches that possessed horses and cattle grazing and running in the field, but none were as magnificent as the RFK Ranch.

"I forgot how beautiful this part of the country is," Nikki said. "The air is so fresh and clean out here."

"I know," Dr. Baker answered. "I love it here. I can't imagine living anywhere else."

"Where do you live, Doc?"

"I live on the ranch," Dr. Baker answered nonchalantly.

"I bet your wife enjoys it."

"I'm a widow," Dr. Baker replied. His eyes remained on the road.

"I'm sorry," Nikki said.

"Don't be. You were right; Nancy loved the ranch. The rodeo. She was a local girl, raised over in Calvert. She went to college, became a nurse, returned home, and came to work at my private practice. That is how we met. Fell in love. Married. Raised a daughter. When Franklin Sr. asked me to head the center, well…" His voice trailed off.

"She came with you." Nikki finished the sentence for him.

"She worked right up to the day she left this earth. May God bless her soul."

"How did she die?"

"Lymphoma."

"Ever thought of getting married again?"

Dr. Baker chuckled. "Not at all? Once was enough. That and no one can take my Nancy's place."

"One day I hope to experience that kind of love," Nikki replied.

"One day you will," Dr. Baker said. "You're beautiful. Intelligent. I guarantee you will find the right man."

Nikki became quiet. She again focused on looking out the passenger window. "I'm sorry that you had to come all the way into town to pick me up."

"It's okay. We get up around here at the crack of dawn. Somewhere around four a.m."

Nikki leaned back in the seat. "Four a.m. I am used to getting up but not that early."

"Cowboys. There are lots of things to do on a ranch."

"Like?" Nikki asked.

"Like branding cattle, breaking horses rounding up animals, baling hay, feeding cattle, mucking stalls, vaccinating calves, and digging wells, to name a few jobs. RFK is also a guest ranch. People come from all over the world to experience what you are getting for free."

"I should be so lucky." Nikki panicked and slid down in the seat. "They don't expect me to do any of the chores, do they?" she asked. "I'm a doctor. I'm not a cowgirl."

"Of course not," Dr. Baker answered. "It takes years of experience to do what those guys do. Your work is in the center and no place else. It's not as prestigious and busy as the hospital, but it keeps us on our toes," he explained. "We see twenty to thirty people a night at the competitions, and, on average, about fifty people at the center. We not only treat the cowboys, we also see their families, staff members, and guests of the ranch. We see everything from stiff muscles to broken bones. The center is full service and the best in the country," he said. "Heck, we also treat the animals."

"Then there is a vet on staff?" Nikki asked.

"We have several vets. It's a staff of sixty. We all came to the clinic by different venues. We have former riders, trainers, and some who just wanted a career change. But they are all hard-working, dedicated doctors. We love what we do."

"Do you travel?"

"Only when the Kincaid's are competing," Dr. Baker explained. "We work the local, state, and national events. No need to worry; you won't break the terms of your service. You may even get to like it around here."

"I doubt it," Nikki said. "I'm a surgeon. I do my best work in the operating room."

"I know," Dr. Baker said. "That's what Dr. Anderson said about you. You were one of the hospital's best doctors. You are cool under pressure. An ice princess. You will fit right in around here."

Nikki's head snapped in Dr. Baker's direction. She swallowed the lump in her throat. "I guess he filled you in on what happened."

"He did," Dr. Baker replied.

"And?"

"I don't give a damn, he had it coming," Dr. Baker quipped as they turned off onto the familiar road she was on last night. She noticed Ross upon his horse, giving instructions to the hired hands, repairing the damaged fence. She frowned and rolled her eyes. It was too early in the morning to deal with him. She had never met a man that infuriated her more than Winston.

"I hear that Ross is a pretty good rodeo rider."

"Pretty good? He is the man to beat right now. National champion the past three years."

"Is that why he's so arrogant?"

Dr. Baker chuckled. He stopped the vehicle and let down the window. Ross got off the horse and strolled toward them.

"Good morning, Doc," he said. His gentle expression dropped when he recognized Nikki in the passenger seat. He touched the brim of his brown Lucchese cap. "Ma'am."

Nikki did not bother to return the greeting. If he was affected by her reaction, he did not show it. Not that she cared.

Ross refocused on Dr. Baker. "Headed to the clinic?"

"Yes. It's her first day. I am going to show her around and introduce her to the other members of the team. Will I see you today?"

"What for?"

"You know what for. I need to take a look at you before the Invitational."

"I'll come see you, Doc," Ross said. "Simmer down."

"Make sure you do," Dr. Baker replied. "Call me."

"We will talk later," Ross said, walking away from the vehicle without another word.

Dr. Baker shook his head. "Geez, that boy is stubborn, just like his ole man."

"I can believe that."

Dr. Baker maneuvered the car expertly along the winding road. She looked over to see a group of beautiful horses running wild. "Wow, what a sight. I have to take photos."

"Yes, they are," Dr. Baker said. "You will have plenty of time for that. Do you ride?"

"The closest I have come to a horse is on television." Nikki giggled.

Dr. Baker burst out laughing. "You should learn while you're here." He pulled the vehicle into a private parking spot. She looked out the window and stretched her eyes. The clinic was not at all what she'd envisioned. What she saw was what looked like a llarge, white, three-level-complex. A triangular roof sat atop the building. A large sycamore tree hung over one side, and a black marble statue of a cowboy throwing a lasso around a calf stood out front.

Nikki read the sign on the building. "The Gallop Clinic."

"The clinic was founded by Franklin Sr. after he was injured and had to leave the rodeo circuit," Dr. Baker explained. "He had to rehab in another state because there wasn't a facility close to home to take care of him." He exited the car. He came around and opened the passenger-side door for Nikki, and then removed a box of files from the backseat. They headed up the sidewalk and toward the building.

"Howdy, folks," a loud voice said behind them. They turned to see a slim young man running to catch up with them. Upon closer examination, he looked to be in his early twenties. "Let me take that off your hands, Doc." He nodded toward Nikki. "Ma'am." The cowboy hat looked too large for his small head.

"Mornin', Simon," Dr. Baker said. "What are you doing here? I don't remember you having an appointment."

"I need to have my hand checked out," Simon said. "It's still hurtin' me somethin' awful."

"Simon, I told you that it is just scar tissue. Just keep clenching and unclenching your fist throughout the day and it will get better," Dr. Baker said as they walked inside the clinic.

"Nice," Nikki replied. She looked around the reception area. The interior was pleasant, airy, light, and attractive. The waiting room was spacious and equipped with plenty of chairs. An LCD television was mounted on one side of the wall. One the other side were pictures of famous cowboys, cowgirls, and rodeo athletes.

Simon looked Nikki up and down. "Who's this pretty lady?"

"Where are my manners?" Dr. Baker said. "Simon Long, this is Dr. Nicole Phillips. She is going to be working in the clinic for a couple of weeks."

"I heard 'bout you," Simon replied. "You're the one that knocked down the fence, right?"

"Does the whole town know about me?" Nikki asked.

Dr. Baker and Simon nodded. "Yep!" They answered in unison.

"It's a small town. I heard you were a looker," Simon continued. "And a doctor, too. You can take this boy's temp anytime."

"Down, boy," Dr. Baker scolded. "Put the box on the desk and go wait in the waiting room. Go on."

Simon set the files on the counter and took a seat in front of the television. He removed his hat and ran a hand through his curly brown hair.

Nikki couldn't help but notice that men from Texas were forward. They were not afraid to say what was on their mind. She liked it; even if she did not like what was said, she knew where she stood.

Her mind drifted to Ross. She could not stand the sight of him, but what she did know of his personality was that he came across as forward and aggressive. She wondered if he was that type of lover. She pushed the thought aside. What was she thinking? There was no way in hell that she would ever be interested in a man like Ross Kincaid. Not even if he were the last man on earth.

"Becky, make Simon an appointment to see me," Dr. Baker said to the receptionist.

"Sure thing, Dr. Baker." The young woman glanced curiously from Nikki to Dr. Baker.

"Becky Sue, this is Dr. Nicole Phillips, a doctor from D.C. She's going to be with us for the next couple of weeks." He turned to Nikki. "Dr. Phillips this is Becky Sue Crawford, our Receptionist. She keeps everything running smoothly around here."

"I know how great Receptionists can be," Nikki said. She extended a hand to the young lady. "It's nice meeting you, Becky Sue."

"Good to meet you," Becky Sue replied. "Welcome. If you need anything, just let me know."

"Thanks."

"I'm going to give Dr. Phillips a quick tour and then start seeing patients," Dr. Baker said. He led her down the hall. As they strolled through the clinic, he pointed out the four wings—outpatient department, rehabilitation, operating rooms, and accommodations suites. All the units in the clinic were cutting-edge. He ended the trip by taking her to the Radiology department.

Dr. Baker led her back to the receptionist desk. "Well, what do you think?"

"I'm very impressed," Nikki replied. "It's more modern than I imagined it would be." She noticed a tall, stunning, statuesque blonde wearing stylish red-framed glasses and a white hospital coat laughing and chatting with Becky Sue. The women hushed as they approached.

"Ahh there you are," Dr. Baker said, heading toward the two ladies. "Dr. Phillips, this is Dr. Vicki Palumbo, the chiropractor for the clinic. She is the best back cracker in the business."

"Thank you for that, Dr. Baker. You're Dr. Phillips from D.C." Dr. Palumbo said. "Everyone has been talking about you."

"I heard. Guilty as charged," Nikki replied.

"Dr. Phillips was born and raised in Montgomery," Dr. Baker said, "so she is a home bred Texan."

"How did you wind up in D.C.?"

"After medical school I took a job there."

"Nice," Dr. Palumbo replied. "I had a chance to take a position at Emory in Atlanta, Georgia. I am a country girl through and through. City life ain't for this gal. This the best job I ever had. You will enjoy it while you're here."

"Most young people leave Norstrom for bigger things, but they always find their way back to Norstrom," Becky Sue said. She handed Dr. Palumbo a chart.

"If you need help with anything, just give me a shout." Dr. Palumbo walked out to the waiting room and called her next patient.

"Everyone seems so helpful around here." Nikki said.

"They are. It is no pretense" Dr. Baker said.

"There you are," Junior replied, walking up to the desk with a sloppy grin on his face.

"What brings you here, Junior?" Dr. Baker asked.

Junior fixed his gaze on Nikki. "I came to see how the new doctor was settling in on her first day." He winked. "Southern hospitality."

Dr. Baker chuckled. "I see. There was no need to come all the way here. I'm more than capable of helping Dr. Phillips settle in."

"I know you can, Doc. That is not the only reason. Father wants to meet the new doctor. He ordered me to invite the kind lady to supper."

Nikki was surprised. "Supper?"

"Yes. Father likes to meet new staff members from the clinic."

"I don't know," Nikki said. She was not comfortable around the wealthy and felt out of her comfort zone. She just wanted to complete her community service and leave Norstrom quietly.

Her mind drifted to how she was unable to fall asleep in the lumpy queen-size bed. She tossed and turned all night. She flopped on her back, looking up into the darkness to try and figure out what her next move should be. There were plenty of local hospitals she could apply to. With her experience and background, she was sure that she would be able to get hired.

"You may as well say yes," Dr. Baker chimed in. "He pays your salary."

"I'm not getting paid," Nikki reminded him.

Dr. Baker leaned over and whispered, "But he's in charge of your community service. You'd better show up."

"What time is dinner?" Nikki inquired.

"The Kincaid's sit down to supper at seven o'clock."

"You have a set time to eat?"

"Father's rule. When we are home, we eat together."

Nikki could not help but feel a little envious. With her and Winston's hectic schedule, they rarely had a chance to have dinner together often. "I'll be there."

"I'll make sure that she is there," Dr. Baker said. "Now get out of here so we can get to work."

Junior was grinning from ear-to-ear. "All right. I'll see you later. Seven o'clock." He turned and hurried back out the door.

Dr. Baker chuckled. "Look like you have an admirer."

"He's just being nice."

Dr. Baker looked at her in disbelief. "If you say so." He clasped his hands together. "Let's get at it."

✳ ✳ ✳

Ross found shade under a giant oak tree. He sat down and opened a bottled water. The liquid vanished in no time. He pulled out a blue bandana and wiped the sweat from his face. It had been a busy morning. He helped pen the cattle, worked the babies and separated those that were to be sold at the market. The Kincaid's were known for raising high-class stock. He made sure that that did not change.

He strolled over toward Bullet. He untied him and rode over to check on the progress of the fence. As he galloped, his mind drifted to Nikki. He did not understand why she came to mind. He could not deny she looked lovely. Fresh as early morning dew. He liked the way her shoulder-length black hair framed her light-brown oval face. The shape of her thin lips stayed on his mind. If she were his woman, he could imagine how much he would enjoy kissing her. Ross pushed the foolish thoughts aside. Nikki could never be his woman. They did not like each other, and that would never change. In two weeks, she would be done with community service and out of his life.

Ross looked up to see Lena heading in his direction on Stardust, a Quarter Horse she raised from birth. She smiled.

"Howdy, Lena." He tipped the end of his hat.

"Ross. How are you doing this morning?"

"Better than I've ever been," Ross answered. "You're up early."

"Not really. I stopped by to thank you for coming to Dad's birthday party. I know you hate that sort of stuff."

Ross leaned forward in the saddle. "I enjoyed myself. It was a special occasion. Where you headed?"

"Wherever you are?"

"I'm headed out to the fence."

"The one the out of towner tore down," Lena said.

"That is the one," Ross said, leading Bullet in the direction of the hired hands.

"Rumors has it she's working at the Gallop," Lena said, riding next to Ross. "I heard it from Clyde. He was in court the same day she was."

"I see," Ross answered. "What trouble did he cause this time?"

"Same ole thing, drunk and disorderly," Lena said. "I know he's my uncle, but this is tuckering me out. Dad keeps telling him if he can't hold his liquor he shouldn't drink, but he ain't listening."

"You know Clyde ain't been the same since Eileen left him."

"I know, but the family has had enough bailing his sorry self out of jail," Lena said. "Clyde told me she's pretty," she said, looking over at Ross.

"Who?"

"The out of towner." Lena said.

"She's okay," Ross answered. He knew that Lena was trying to figure out how he felt about the new worker. As far as he was concerned, there was nothing to be worried about.

"How long is she going to be here?"

"Two weeks at the most," Ross answered.

"That is a long time," Lena replied in a low tone.

"Well, it wasn't my idea," Ross replied. "Good old Judge Spears figures that is how long it will take for her to pay for the damages to the fence."

"Wouldn't you know it," Lena said. "She's a criminal."

"I wouldn't call her a criminal." Ross said. "Just rude as hell."

"No home training," Lena said. "I'm not surprised."

They looked to see Junior parked on the private road. He quickly exited the truck and jumped the fence with ease. "Lena, girl, you are still as beautiful as ever." He kissed her on the cheek.

"Flattery will get you everywhere." Lena beamed. "Where are you coming from in such a hurry?"

"From the clinic. We got a new lady doctor," Junior answered. "I wanted to make sure that she was all settled in."

Lena chuckled. "She must be some woman to get such treatment. I have to meet her."

"She's a lovely little filly. Smart. Pretty. Feisty." Junior threw his hat up in the air. "Just the way I like 'em.

Ross sighed. "This guy."

Junior shrugged. "What?"

Ross leaned slightly forward in the saddle. "How is the good doctor doing?"

"She's doing just fine," Junior answered. "Father invited her to supper tonight."

Lena's smile slipped. "Supper? Tonight?"

"It's Dad's way of getting to know the new employees," Junior explained. "He does it for all workers at the Gallop."

"And I bet you're hoping to benefit from good ole Dad's policy," Ross said. "I still think you are barking up the wrong tree. She is out of your league."

Junior ignored Ross's remark. He refocused on Lena. "Why don't you come to supper too? I know Dad would love to see you. He asks about you all the time, and he won't mind you dropping in."

Lena glanced over at Ross. "I think that is a splendid idea. I can't wait to meet the good doctor."

"Good," Junior answered. "You know we sit down to supper at seven o'clock."

"I will see you boys then." Lena nudged Stardust and galloped off.

"I just made her day," Junior said as he watched her disappear in the distance.

Ross remained silent, then quickly headed in the opposite direction.

* * *

Nikki's first day at the clinic passed quickly. Not only did she treat bone injuries, but she also treated non-orthopedic patients. It reminded her of her residence days when she worked the emergency room. She treated everything from an adult broken arm to a two-year-old's earache. It felt good to go back to the time when her life was less eventful.

"You did well your first day," Dr. Baker replied. "How do you feel?"

"I feel good. It reminded me of my residence days," Nikki answered. She walked over to the sink to sanitize and wash her hands. "It's been a while since I did general practice, but I guess it never goes away."

"No, it doesn't," Dr. Baker said. "You never forget." He strolled over and stood next to her. His face became serious. "Can I ask you something?"

Nikki grabbed a paper towel and dried her hands. "Sure."

"Watching you today, you looked comfortable. You were wonderful with the patients. They seem to take to you. It was good to see you smile. What made you decide to go into orthopedics?"

Nikki sighed. "My ex-fiancé." She leaned against the examination table. "He thought it was a good idea for the future Mrs. Thorpe to also be an orthopedic surgeon. We were going to be a power couple. Look how that turned out."

Dr. Baker rubbed his chin. "What were you initially thinking of as a specialty?"

She crossed her arms across her chest. "Pediatric, maybe? Obstetrics was another I considered. I wanted to work with kids and babies."

"I guess that's why you were a big hit with the little ones today." Dr. Baker glanced at his watch, "You were a natural. I have a late appointment scheduled. Do you mind waiting? Or do you want me to call Junior? I'm sure he won't mind driving you home."

"I'll wait for you outside," Nikki answered.

"It won't take long," Dr. Baker replied as he escorted her to the front of the clinic. Everyone was gone for the day. It was quiet. "I'll give you a call when I'm done."

Nikki felt like she was being pushed out the door. "I'll wait for your call." She headed into the staff dressing room, changed out of the scrubs, and grabbed her purse out of her locker.

Dr. Baker unlocked the front door to allow her to exit. She casually strolled out of the clinic down the sidewalk, and to the front of the building. She made her way over to the bench underneath the large oak tree and sat down. Her feet were killing her.

She looked up at the clear blue sky. The sunrays beamed down on her face. She closed her eyes, soaking in the ambiance of RFK. The sound of a twig snapped her out of her thoughts. With the brightness in her face, she couldn't make out the tall silhouette. She raised a hand to block the sun. "Who is it?"

"You should wear shades to protect your eyes," the person said.

Nikki recognized the deep, sultry voice as belonging to Ross. "Oh, it's you," she said in disappointment. "My eyes are none of your business."

He was chewing a straw of yellow grass. "I never said it was my business. Just some friendly advice, that's all."

"Hrump," Nikki said. "Friendly? You don't know the meaning of the word."

"Can't we just do this whole thing over?" Ross prompted. "Since you are going to be working here, we should try and get along."

"Wow," Nikki gasped. "You have some nerve. If it was not for you, I would not be in this one-horse town, so I have no intention of being civil toward you. I don't even want to talk to you."

Ross slightly spread his legs apart and folded his arms across his broad chest. "I don't care if you never speak to me or not. That is your business; I was just giving advice because it can get terribly hot here in Norstrom."

"I'm a doctor," Nikki hissed. "I think I know something about dealing with the heat."

"Then where is your water? Light clothing?" Ross fired question after question. "Are you wearing sunscreen to protect your skin?" Without giving her a chance at a comeback he walked off, giving himself the last word.

Nikki watched him stroll off with confidence. "Jerk," She mouthed. She turned around to see Dr. Baker opening the door for Ross. He must be his late appointment. She could not help but wonder why he was meeting him after hours.

* * *

Dr. Baker looked at the results from Ross's MRI. "It won't prevent you from riding, but it's not healing as fast as it should. That worries me. I don't think you should compete in the Invitational," Dr. Baker explained. "Matter of fact, you should take some time off. Give your body a rest."

Ross slipped one arm into the shirt and then the other. "Doc, I have followed your instructions. I have been very careful."

"Ross, you have nothing to prove to anyone; you are on top. No African-American has achieved as much and done it in the short amount of time as you have."

"No one knows that better than me."

Dr. Baker removed the stethoscope from around his neck. "Then move on with your life."

"What are you talking about?" Ross snapped the buttons on his shirt with extra force.

"Ross, I know how you felt about Hailey. You loved her. She hurt you. I get it, but that is no reason to go out and compete like this knowing one wrong fall could paralyze you. It's just not worth it."

Ross dipped his head. "It's all I have."

"That's not true. You have a family that loves you. You have this great guest ranch. You have been lucky so far, don't chance it."

Ross cleared his throat. "Are we done, Doc?"

Dr. Baker tossed the stethoscope on the desk out of frustration. "Yeah, we're done. You can leave now."

"I can compete in the Invitational?"

Dr. Baker plopped down in the chair, his back to Ross. He shook his head. "Yes. There is nothing I can do but tell you to be careful."

"Don't worry, Doc," Ross replied. "I will be careful. I'm not going to end up in a wheelchair or worse." He slapped him on the back.

"Ross?" Dr. Baker began, then thought better of it.

Ross did not miss the worried expression on the doctor's face. "Doc, I heard what you said." He turned and walked out the door.

* * *

Nikki opened the Gucci luggage bag to choose something to wear. She picked up an ugly tan dress and tossed it aside. Just what do you wear to dinner at a ranch? She and Winston had often dined with upscale friends, but she had no idea what to wear to dinner with the Kincaid's. She glanced at the dark-blue pants suit and tossed it back in the bag. Overkill. When she left D.C., she didn't think about packing clothes for a dinner, on a ranch, and with a rich family.

Nikki ran a hand down her face in frustration. She wondered if there was a mall nearby. She did not remember passing one in town. She glanced at her watch; it was four o'clock. Dinner was at seven. If she hurried, she might able to purchase an outfit for the occasion.

She grabbed her clutch purse off the bed and started toward the door. The ringing of the cellular phone stopped her in her tracks. She looked in the bag and recognized Corina's number. She smiled. They had not spoken since she left D.C.

She answered the call. "It's about time you phoned," Nikki teased. "I was beginning to think that you forgot about me."

"Uh, that works both ways. How can you resign? Leave town and not tell me?" Corina squealed. "Your best friend. Remember, your partner in crime. I couldn't believe it," she continued. "I came to work the next day and was told that you were no longer at the hospital. Talk about a shock. Why didn't you call and tell me what happened? I have been frantic."

Nikki sat on the edge of the bed. "I just couldn't. I was so angry and upset at the time. I just wanted to get away."

"I'm sorry. What happened?"

She told Corina about the day she was let go.

"Oh, sweetie, I'm so sorry. Winston is such an ass. How could he do something like that?"

"Well, he did. How is everyone doing?" Nikki asked.

"What do you mean by everyone?"

Silence fell between them.

"Don't tell me you are still thinking of that jerk Winston?"

She was embarrassed. "No. I was just wondering how everyone was doing. Who is covering my patients?"

"Everyone is fine. Dr. Penn is seeing a majority of them over sixty-five. But he divided the children and adults amongst the other providers."

"David?" Nikki inquired.

"David is looking into your dismissal. He says that he is going to fight to get your job back," Corina relayed. "I believe he can do it. You will be back here in no time. You should forgive him. He really is sorry for not telling you."

"I'm surprise to hear you take his side," Nikki said.

"I know but, he is speaking on your behalf," Corina said. "I admire him for that. Don't you want to come back?"

Nikki scowled. She missed Bayside but was not sure if she wanted to return. "Maybe. I am not sure. I'm not going to rule anything out."

"Think about it. We all miss you."

"I will."

"What about David?"

"In due time," Nikki said. "We have been friends for a long time. I'm just mad at him right now."

"That's good to hear. Enough of that," Corina said. "How are you? The family?"

Nikki chuckled. "I'm fine. I can't say about my family; I haven't made it to Montgomery."

Corina gasped. "What do you mean? Where are you?"

"I'm stuck in Norstrom for the next two weeks."

"Come again?" Corina inquired. "Norstrom? Where is that?"

"It's a small town about one-hundred-and-fifty-miles outside of Houston," Nikki relayed.

"Okay," Corina said. "You'd better explain. What is going on?"

Nikki told her friend everything that had transpired within the last twenty-four hours.

"You have to do two weeks of community service to pay for the damages on a ranch full of cowboys?" Corina asked.

"Can you believe it?" Nikki asked. "Talk about a nightmare."

"Sounds dreamy to me."

Nikki tossed her shoulder length, black hair over her shoulder. "The ranch itself is beautiful. I mean, it's like a page out of Mansion Homes Magazine. The guest ranch is great. Lots to do and take advantage of."

"Sounds like a place I have to visit."

"And then there is Ross Kincaid."

"The cowboy that had you arrested." Corina giggled. "Sounds like a lot of hot, sizzling chemistry going on between you two."

"What? Come on, Corina. The man had me arrested."

"That's his way of getting your attention." Corina laughed. "Sounds to me like he may be able to tame that attitude of yours."

"What attitude?" Nikki asked. "Winston never thought I had an attitude. Matter-of-fact, he loved that I was an independent woman."

"Then he left you for another woman, who's just the opposite."

Nikki's heart stopped a moment. Corina's words hurt, but they were true. "Ouch. For the record, I met the new woman. She's not a pushover. It's doesn't matter; there's no way that Ross and I will ever get together.

His brother, Junior, is more my type. Handsome. Attentive. Caring. I like that in a man."

"Someone you can control," Corina threw in.

"That's not true."

"Isn't it?"

"No, it isn't."

"If you say so."

"Besides, I don't think any woman can control Junior," Nikki said. "He seems to be the type to do what he wants when he wants."

"Like his brother, Ross." Corina said.

"Junior thinks he is a womanizer and Ross is just the opposite."

"But Junior is your type?" Corina inquired.

"I'm not looking for a type," Nikki confessed. "I haven't gotten over what happened with Winston. I have a feeling it's going to be a while before I do."

"That's why the ranch is right for you right now. The change of pace will do you good."

"You're right," Nikki agreed. "I guess. I don't know."

"Who would have ever thought you would be working on a ranch?" Corina replied. "Full of hot, hunky cowboys. I am so envious of you right now."

"Not me."

Nikki laughed and spoke with Corina a few more minutes. She made her way downstairs and found Miss Mabelle in the dining room clearing off the tables. She was fussing up a storm. "Good for nothing, young'un. I bet he's up at The Big Boot." She was mumbling to herself.

"It's Friday night," an older man said. He shoveled a spoonful of mashed potatoes in his mouth. "Folks like to dance, ride the mechanical bull, and latch on to some little filly."

"You mean act a fool." The man across from him burst out laughing. "I know that's what I used to do." He coughed and almost fell off the stool he was sitting on. "Yep, I'm crazy about The Big Boot. My favorite drinking hole. The little lady had to bail me out of jail many times because of that place." His eyes fell on Nikki standing at the counter. "You lost, little lady?"

All the heads in the room turned to Nikki.

"Oh, hey, Doc," Mabelle said, wiping her short, stubby hand on her white apron.

Nikki said awkwardly, "Miss Mabelle."

"It's Mrs. I'm a widow." She walked back behind the counter and waited on the next customer.

Nikki gulped. "I'm sorry about your loss."

"It's okay, sugar. I lost my Frank five years ago," Mabelle explained. "It's been a struggle." She lovingly smiled. "But I have my memories, and I'm doing just fine. I'm sorry, I didn't mean to go on so."

"Oh, it's okay. I'm a good listener," Nikki joked to lighten the mood.

"I been meaning to ask you about last night when Dr. Baker dropped you off," Mabelle said. "What kind of doctor are ya?"

"She's a heart doctor," the man at the counter answered for her.

"I heard one of those women doctors," another man coming up to the counter added to the conversation. "Mabelle, give me a piece of that apple pie of yours," he said and winked at Mabelle. "I swear, old gurl, if I weren't already married I would make you my wife."

Nikki couldn't believe the conversation going on around her. They were talking about her as if she weren't there.

Mabelle threw her head back and laughed. "Forget about it, Jube. You had your chance. Besides, I like 'em young and tender."

Jube refocused on Nikki. "Ma'am, what kind of doctor are you?"

"I'm an orthopedist."

Everyone at the counter mumbled.

"A what?" Jube inquired in a deep southern drawl.

Nikki had to remember she was. People were a little slower than those in the city. She had to put it in simple terms. "I'm a bone doctor."

"You're in the right town," Jube replied. "If it's one thing Norstrom is known for, it's broken bones."

Everyone laughed.

"You can say that again," Mabelle joked.

The older man sitting at the counter began to cough again. Nikki looked at him with a concerned expression on her face. She didn't like the sound coming from his chest. "Have you seen a doctor for that cough?"

"Why do you ask?"

"It doesn't sound right. You should get it checked out," Nikki replied. "Especially a man of your age. No offense."

Mabelle waved a hand in mid-air. "We've been trying to get old Zack here to see someone for months. He won't go. Says there is no reason to see one. Don't worry about it; he will be okay. What can I do for you? Are you hungry? Can I get you something to eat?"

"No. I'm headed out to dinner," Nikki replied. "I was just wondering if there was a mall nearby. I need to buy a dress."

They laughed again.

Nikki was embarrassed. "What's so funny?"

"You are a city girl," Mabelle said in a thick Texas drawl. "The nearest mall is in the next county. That's about twenty miles away."

Nikki couldn't believe her ears. twenty miles? She didn't know what she would do without weekly shopping trips to the mall. Her life was made for sales, especially shoes. She tilted her head to one side and collected her thoughts. "Can you recommend a boutique? Dress shop? Something like that."

"We ain't living in the Stone Age," Mabelle said with sarcasm. "We have those shops." She ran a hand over her full figure. "Of course, I don't go in for those girly things myself, but there are a couple of shops like that at the end of the square." She pointed. "Just head out, make a left, and walk to the end of the block. You can't miss 'em."

"Thank you." Nikki hiked her purse up on her shoulder. She hurried out the door. Following Mabelle's directions, she reached her destination within five minutes. It gave her a chance to look around Norstrom. There were several specialty shops, hardware stores, restaurants, a library, and a cell phone store. She walked a few more steps and found herself standing in front of Melanie's Beauty & Nails. Next to it was Her Style Boutique.

Nikki peeped through the large-paned window of the beauty shop. There were attendants busy moving about between customers. A young girl in her mid-twenties with short red hair walked outside and waved her in. "Step on in." She opened the door wider, coaxing her in. "You must be the doctor."

Nikki shouldn't be surprised, but she was. "I am the doctor."

The girl grinned. "Everybody in Norstrom knows everybody, so when someone new is in town, we are all aware. Besides, you are kind of famous."

"Famous?"

"Yeah. The woman doctor that knocked down the Kincaid's fence."

Nikki's cheeks burned. "I don't see how that makes me famous. But whatever you say."

The young lady extended a hand. "I'm Lilly."

"Lilly?" Nikki prompted.

"Just Lilly."

"Okay, just Lilly. Maybe you can help me."

"I'll try."

"I need to buy a dress for dinner."

Lilly frowned. "You're going purchase a dress for dinner? We don't usually get all gussied up to eat unless it's for a special occasion." Her eyes lit up. "Is it a romantic dinner?"

"No. It's nothing like that."

Lilly placed a hand on her thin hip. "Junior is going to be disappointed."

Nikki eyes stretched. "Junior? What does he have to do with anything?"

The other women in the shop turned in their direction. Lilly whispered, "Word is you two are courting? You know, dating," she explained.

"I know what it means. Junior and I are not dating," Nikki emphasized. "I barely know the man. I'm only having dinner with the Kincaid family; that's it." She didn't understand why she felt she had to explain her actions to the women in the shop. "It's a rule of Mr. Kincaid Sr. to meet all the new employees."

Nikki heard groans around the room.

"She is telling the truth," Nikki heard a woman's voice say from the back of room. A stunning African-American woman with long black hair, dressed in a two-piece denim skirt suit and black cowboy boots, walked confidently toward the checkout. As she came closer, Nikki couldn't help but notice her perfect cocoa brown complexion and exquisite, chiseled face. She appeared to be in her mid-twenties. Her makeup flawless. She didn't usually feel intimidated by other women, but this one put her to shame.

The woman paid the bill and went and stood in front of her. "You must be Nikki." She extended a petite, manicured hand.

Nikki accepted the handshake. It was smooth and soft to the touch. She shouldn't be surprised. The woman looked like she could afford the best. "Yes. I'm Dr. Nicole Phillips."

"I'm Lena Spaulding. My family owns the ranch next to the Kincaid's."

Nikki bobbed her head up and down in acknowledgement. That explains her high-class persona, she said to herself.

"I have heard so much about you; I'm glad I finally got a chance to meet you," Lena said.

Nikki arched an inquisitive eyebrow. "You heard about me from?"

"Junior of course," Lena answered. "He was raving about you today to Ross and me when we were out riding."

Lilly rolled her eyes toward the ceiling.

"Oh, I see." Nikki did not understand why, but her heart dropped at the thought of her being with Ross.

"Do you ride?" Lena inquired.

"No, I don't," Nikki answered.

"You should get Junior to teach you while you're here. He is very good. Though he's not as good as Ross."

Nikki could not help but notice how her eyes lit up when she spoke about Ross. Were they a couple? She didn't look his type. Lena appeared high maintenance. She reminded her of Alessa Coffer. The woman that came between her and Winston. Because she had money, she always got what she wanted.

"Ross is the best bull rider in the country," Lena bragged.

"I heard," Nikki replied. "Do you compete?" She really didn't care. She was just making conversation.

Lena's face broke into a big smile. "I am a three-time national champion in barrel racing. I also compete in women's roping, and I train high-caliber horses." She raised her nose in the air. "Thanks for asking."

Not only was Lena beautiful, but she was also athletic. It was official; Nikki didn't like her.

"You should try it," Lena challenged. "Even a city girl like you can do it."

Nikki blinked. Was this young girl challenging her? She was a surgeon. She graduated second in her class. She trained for over ten years to become the best in her field. Why would she want to race around a barrel? Ridiculous. "No, thank you, I'll leave that to you."

Lena smirked. "Yes, you should."

Nikki sensed Lena was enjoying pushing her buttons. But why was she baiting her? They didn't know each other.

"I have to get going," Lena said. She threw up a hand to Lilly. "We will chat later at dinner."

Nikki frowned. She hoped she didn't mean what she thought she meant. "At dinner?"

"Yes, I'll be Ross's date dinner date this evening. I'll see you then." She walked out the door without a backward glance.

The ladies in the shop began mumbling after her exit.

"She is something else," Lilly exclaimed.

"That woman knows how to get tongues wagging where ever she goes," another woman said, coming from one of the back rooms. She placed her hands on her hips. Her fiery-red hair was piled neatly atop her head, matched the lipstick on her thin lips.

Nikki admired the blue-and-white denim dress. The designer brown cowgirl boots were breathtaking. She couldn't help but notice everyone in Norstrom was dressed in Western attire. She was feeling out of place. "I love your outfit. Where did you get it?"

"Little shop called The Barn. It's next door," the woman answered. "They carry all of the latest in cowboy and girl fashion. Reasonable prices. Outfits for every occasion. Great selections."

"Thank you," Nikki said.

"Misty Dudley." The woman extended a hand. "I'm the owner of this shop." She looked at Nikki's head. "Looks like you came just in the nick of time. Your roots are sprouting like weed."

Nikki self-consciously ran a hand through her hair. "Yeah, I think I need the works. Wash, set, deep conditioning."

"I'll say," Misty replied. "What about those hands?"

Nikki looked at her fingernails. Because of her profession, it had been a while since she'd had them done. Whenever she and Corina did attend a beauty shop, it was mostly to get her hair and feet done. "I would like to have them done."

Misty smiled. "Norstrom is a town of good people, like Lilly said. Don't mind Lena. The rich always act that way. It wouldn't have matter if you were from the big city or out here in the wide-open country, she still would have been rude. But I don't have to tell you that."

"No, you don't," Nikki said. "What is her problem?"

"Ross Kincaid," Lilly chimed in.

"Ross?" Nikki repeated. "What about him?"

"Lena has been in love with him since, like, forever," Lilly explained. "Everyone in Norstrom knows it."

"She doesn't hide it," Nikki replied.

"Folks say that Lena is the reason Ross and his ex-fiancée, Hailey broke up," Lilly continued.

"Oh, hush up," Misty chimed in. "That's just talk."

Nikki pepped up. Ross was engaged? She wanted to know more about what happened between Ross and his ex. With his personality, she was surprised that women found him attractive. She guessed there was no accounting for taste. He didn't appear to be the loving and caring type, like Junior.

Lilly shrugged. "I'm just saying that is the rumor." She refocused on Nikki.

"Well it is a stupid rumor," Misty said, changing the subject. "Will you be attending the Sweet Bronco Invitational?"

"I guess so," Nikki answered awkwardly. "If I am still in town."

"You should come. I just know that Ross is going to win it all again," Lilly said with confidence.

"Not this year," a woman said, settling underneath a dryer. "J.D. is taking it this year."

"Kincaid is a natural-born rider," a nail technician threw in. "There is no way that J.D. is taking him off the throne."

Nikki looked around the dress shop in awe. It was the same as Mabelle's. The customers were passionate about who they felt would beat Ross for the title. "I guess I have to get use to this."

"You'll get used to it. How do you want your hair done?" Misty asked. Wavy? Keep it long? Or cut it short?"

"Let's put some waves to it," Nikki said. "Just a quick wash and set." She found herself wondering if Ross would like the new look.

* * *

"Have all of the calves been branded?" Franklin Sr. asked, strolling in the barn. He placed both hands on his hips, legs slightly apart.

"Finished it this morning," Blake answered.

"Where are your brothers?" Franklin Sr. craned his neck, searching for Ross and Junior.

"They headed over to the resort to check on things. Business has picked up in the past couple of weeks. They should be back in time for supper."

"Good to hear," Franklin Sr. said. "What can you tell me about the new doctor? Dr. Phillips," he asked out of the blue. "Our invited guest."

Blake pushed the hat back on his head and stuck his fingers in his belt buckle. "Not much, except she's pretty."

Franklin Sr. chuckled. "That's all you would see. Where is she from?"

"She says she has kin in Montgomery."

"Phillips? Phillips? I don't think I know her folks," Franklin Sr. said. "Hurry on in the house, clean yourself up, and get ready for supper."

"I'll head on in a minute," Blake answered.

Franklin Sr. strolled out of the barn and then poked his head back in. "Are you bringing someone?"

116

Blake smiled. "I wasn't going to but since Ross will have Lena Spaulding and Junior has taken a liking to Dr. Phillips. I'm guessin' I should."

"It's up to you," Franklin Sr. said over his right shoulder on his way out the door. He shook his head from side to side. He should not be surprised; if there was a lovely woman within one hundred miles, his sons would sniff them out. They reminded him of himself when he was younger, except Ross; he was the most level headed and business-minded of the three. When he was at the ranch, it ran like clockwork; which was why he wanted him to give up competing and run the guest ranch full-time. Maybe then he would be able to settle down and give him grandchildren.

Franklin Sr. strolled across the lawn. He looked to see Ross's black Ford Bronco truck headed toward him. It came to a sudden stop in front of him. He and Junior hopped out.

"Watch your toes, old man," Ross joked.

"Who are you calling old?" Franklin Sr. chuckled. "Any time you want to get on the mechanical bull out back and go a few rounds let dis old man know."

"You didn't get enough of the last whooping I put on ya?" Ross threw back.

Franklin Sr. laughed. "You got lucky, boy. Don't forget that."

"That is how you want to remember it, that's fine with me."

"How are things going at the guest ranch? Blake tells me business is up," Franklin Sr. said, changing the subject.

"Yes. Reservations have more than triple from this same time last year," Junior said, "especially since we added the Real Western Overnight on the Range experience. Folks are choosing that package over all the others. That was a good call, Dad."

"I agree," Ross agreed. "Nothing like spending a night out under the stars; especially with a loved one."

"Tell the truth and shame the devil," Junior replied.

"You guys head on in and get cleaned up," Franklin Sr. suggested. "Folks will be arriving shortly."

Ross frowned.

"What's wrong with your face?" Franklin Sr. asked.

Junior slapped Ross on the back. "He can't wait to see Lena, that's all."

"Well, that's good," Franklin Sr. said. "I'm looking forward to seeing her myself." He waved his sons inside.

"I gotta get showered and dressed. I need to pick up my date," Junior declared.

"I heard you are bringing the new doctor," Franklin Sr. said.

Junior smiled. "Yes, sir."

"You have taken a liking to her, huh?" Franklin Sr. asked.

"A man can't go wrong liking her," Junior answered.

Franklin Sr. chuckled. "Well, be on your way."

"I will see you all later," Junior said, heading upstairs two steps at a time.

"He is as anxious as a June bug in the Spring time," Franklin Sr. said.

Chapter Six

Nikki opened the door to Junior at exactly six o'clock. Dressed in a black silk dress coat, white shirt, skinny tie, and black jeans, he was looking tasty.

Junior looked her up and down. She didn't miss that his brown eyes rested on the low-cut black dress with matching pumps she'd purchased at the dress shop.

She smiled inside. She decided to wear her hair atop her head to accentuate her long neck. Misty had talked her into getting a full makeover. The idea was to get Junior's attention, and she'd done that.

Junior removed his black cowboy hat. "Wow, you look beautiful."

Nikki smiled. "Thank you, Junior. You don't look too shabby yourself."

"I look like a bum next to you. I am under dressed. But I feel like I'm the luckiest man in the world right now." He reached behind his back and presented her with a vase of roses. "These are for you. I know you may not have a vase, so I bought one."

"Good thinking. They are lovely, Junior. How did you know I like roses?"

"All women like roses."

Nikki stepped aside and allowed him to come further into the room. She sniffed the flowers. "I love the scent of fresh roses. I can't remember the last time I received them," she said, walking back into the room. She set the vase on the dresser.

"I find that hard to believe," Junior said. "I'm sure your boyfriend often gave you flowers."

Nikki arranged the bouquet. "Winston wasn't really into romantic gestures. I mean, in the beginning of our relationship, he tried. You know dinner, candlelight, candy, and chocolate now and then, but it wasn't really him."

"That's a shame," Junior said. "You seem like the type of woman who likes to be wined and dined."

"Well, it doesn't hurt." Nikki ran a hand over her well-fitted dress. "You sure I am not over dressed?"

"Darling, you look fine," Junior answered. "That's not what I asked you."

"It may be hard to ride the mechanical bull, but for dinner, you look beautiful."

Nikki blinked. "Mechanical bull? What mechanical bull?

"It was going to be a surprise," Junior said. "I was thinking that after dinner we'd head on over to The Big Boot to let off some steam."

"The Big Boot?" Nikki asked in disbelief. "What is that?"

"It's a hot spot where all of the cowboys and girls hang out. Folks go there to blow off some steam, ride the bull, and kick their heels up with some good ole fashion line dancing." He clasped his hands together in anticipation. "So, you're ready to go?"

"I think I'd better go change," Nikki said, turning toward the bathroom.

Junior grabbed her by the arm. "You bought this beautiful outfit for dinner, so you might as well wear it. If we head over to the club, you can always change later."

"I've only seen that type of dance on television. I didn't realize people still do it." She was amazed. "Line dance. You line dance?"

Junior's expression slipped. "Of course." He guided her out the door and to his truck.

* * *

"What a beauty you are," Franklin Sr. said. "I see why my son is taken with you. Come on in. I am glad you could make it on short notice." He took her by the elbow and guided her into a spacious living room. The luxurious high-quality furniture was designed out of rosewood. She looked up at the chandelier carved in the shape of a wagon wheel. Large wooden beams ran the length of the room. Western-themed photos, paintings, and tapestries hung on the wall. A large moose head hung above the fireplace. A 60-inch LCD television was mounted on the opposite wall. Underneath the TV was a built-in mantle full of family photos.

Nikki's eyes fell on the handsome mature man with the salt- and-pepper hair. She could see where his sons get their good looks. She stopped in front of what looked like an antique handwoven Indian rug. "It's lovely. Exquisite artwork. Is it real?"

Franklin Sr. tried not to laugh. "Damn right it is. It was a gift given to my great-great-grandfather from a Cherokee chief who befriended him for saving his life."

"Really? Who was your great-great-grandfather?"

"Sergeant Robert Franklin Kincaid. He was a buffalo soldier."

"Buffalo soldier?" Nikki replied. "Impressive."

"Damn right he was. He served during the Plains Indian Nightmare," Franklin Sr. continued. "It was during the Civil War at the height of tensions between the soldiers and the Indians."

Nikki nodded in admiration. "I see. I guess that's where the riding began."

Franklin Sr. smirked. "You could say that. My great-great-grandfather was a slave. He ran away from his master and joined the Army. He was good at riding and breaking horses that he was put in charge of taking care of them."

"So, he taught your grandfather, and your father taught you, and you taught your sons. But riding is one thing—where does the rodeo come into it?"

Franklin Sr. escorted her over to the sofa. He took the chair across from her. "My grandfather was close friends with Bill Pickett. Have you heard of him?"

Nikki shook her head.

"He was one of the greatest negro rodeo riders to ever sit on a horse," Franklin Sr. said. "To this day there is a rodeo circuit named after him."

"Really?" Nikki asked.

"Anyway, they often went riding together," Franklin Sr. continued. "Old Bill always bragged about how he was the best rider ever to walk the earth. My granddaddy took offense to that and started competing in the rodeo. It was a rivalry that went on for years until Bill's death. My daddy stayed on the rodeo circuit. I followed in his footsteps until I ran into a bull I couldn't handle and injured my leg." He slapped his right leg. "I had to give it up."

"I'm sorry," Nikki said.

"Don't be," Franklin Sr. replied. "I rode for many years before I was forced to give it up. What do you think of our little clinic?" he suddenly asked.

"I've only been there a day," Nikki said. "But from what I've seen so far it is very impressive. It's more modern than I expected it to be."

"What did you expect?" Franklin Sr. asked. "A one room shack."

"No. Nothing like that," Nikki said. "To be honest, I didn't know what to expect. There were more patients than I thought there would be."

"The clinic not only takes care of the cowboys but the resort's employees and guests. It can get quite busy."

"I found that out," Nikki said.

"Being a sawbones, your folks must be proud," Franklin Sr. said.

"Sawbones?"

"Bone doctor," Junior answered. "Folks like you and Doc Baker."

Nikki chuckled. "While I'm here I have to get used to the Rodeo language."

"I admit we do have jargon of our own, but the thing is, we know what we're talking about." Franklin Sr. laughed. "Blake tells me you're from the area."

"She's from Montgomery," Junior said. "Dad, did you forget that she's my date?"

"Truth be told," Franklin Sr. answered, "I forgot about you, son. I am taken in by her beauty."

"Get your own date," Junior teased.

A moment later, Ross casually walked in the room. Nikki blinked. He cleaned up well. The body his clothes were hanging on should be illegal. He wore denim jeans and a black shirt, open at the top, that fit snugly across his broad chest. The ensemble ended with black cowboy boots and a silver belt buckle with the initials RFK. A heat wave washed over her body. She could not take her eyes off his beautiful, smooth, dark caramel face.

Ross must have felt Nikki staring at him. He glanced over at her and their eyes locked for a moment. Hers quickly skidded away.

"Hello, son," Franklin Sr. said. "I was filling the doctor in on the Kincaid family rodeo legacy."

"I'm sure Dr. Phillips doesn't want to hear about that," Ross replied.

"Honestly, I found it interesting to hear about the Kincaid family tree," Nikki said. "It's a history to be proud of."

Ross leaned back in surprise. "No cowboy jokes?"

Nikki threw her hands up in surrender. "None."

"Don't start, Ross," Junior chimed in.

"Son," Franklin Sr. managed to get in.

Ross strolled across the room to prepare himself a drink. The spur sound of his boots filled the air. "I didn't mean any disrespect," he said. "It's just that the good doctor here has made it clear how she feels about cowboys."

"Not all cowboys," Nikki threw back. Franklin Sr. and Junior laughed.

"She's quick," Franklin Sr. said. "I like that."

Nikki's and Ross's eyes locked again. She didn't want to admit it, but there was an animal magnetism between them. She didn't understand what was happening.

The room fell silent. Junior was the first to break it. He glanced over at Nikki. "Doesn't Nikki look lovely this evening?"

"Yes, she does," Ross confirmed. He gave her a subtle look up and down over the rim of the glass.

"She has my vote," Franklin Sr. said.

"Doc, I—"

"Please call me Nikki," she suggested. "All of my friends do."

"Okay, Nikki," Franklin Sr. answered. "I was going to say that I hope you get a chance to enjoy our little ranch while you're here."

"Little?" Nikki said. "There's nothing little about RFK, from what I've seen so far."

Franklin Sr. focused on his son. "Junior is a bad host; he should have given you a tour of the place. There is much to do and see besides the clinic."

"Dad, she just got here," Junior argued.

"The only place he invited me to so far is the The Big Boot."

Ross chuckled. "That dump."

"That's no place to take a lady," Franklin Sr. agreed.

"I'm with you, Dad," Ross chimed in. "It isn't."

"That's because you can't dance," Junior teased.

"Two left feet," Blake said, coming into the room.

Nikki looked to see Lilly on his arm. "Then we have something in common. I can't dance either." She could have imagined it, but she thought she saw a tight smile cross Ross's face.

"I keep telling him that I would be happy to teach him," Lena answered, following Blake into the room. She strolled over and kissed Franklin Sr. on the cheek. He smiled up at her. "Dad sends his greetings."

"Tell him I'll drop around and see him tomorrow," Franklin Sr. said.

"I'll let him know," Lena replied, tapping him on the hand. She focused on Nikki. "We meet again."

Nikki decided to play nice. "Lena, it's good to see you again." She couldn't help but notice she was dressed in a long, white ruffled Summer dress, short black vest, and cowboy boots. "You look nice."

"Yes, it is." Lena said. She looked her up and down. "Thank you. You look over dressed." She hurried over next to Ross.

"I think she look beautiful," Junior said.

"Dad, where's your date?" Ross said out of the blue.

Franklin Sr. playfully looked at his watch. "I don't know. She's running late."

"How long has this been going on?" Ross said.

"Mr. Kincaid," Lilly began, "Misty said she will call you later with the information you discussed."

The three sons looked at each other in surprise.

"Supper is ready, sir," Chuck announced.

"You heard Chuck," Franklin Sr. said. "Let's eat." He ushered everyone into the dining room.

"What is going on between Dad and Misty?" Ross asked Lilly.

"I don't know," Lilly whispered. "I'm just the messenger."

"I think that's great," Lena said, placing an arm through Ross's as they headed into the dining room. She glanced over her right shoulder at Nikki and smiled.

* * *

"I can't eat another bite," Nikki said. She was full as a tick. "It's been a long time since I have had brisket," she said to Junior as they left the dining room. "That smoky flavor barbecue sauce was to die for."

"Chuck makes the best brisket in the county," Junior said.

"You get no argument from me," Nikki said. "It was delicious."

"I guess you kids are headed out to The Big Boot?" Franklin Sr. said, coming from behind them.

"We're going to dance off the food," Junior replied.

Nikki self-consciously ran a hand over her dress. It was tight after eating. She felt as if it would burst open. "I need to change my clothing."

"We can stop by my place on the way to The Big Boot," Lilly suggested. "We look about the same size. I may have something for you to put on."

"We'll meet you guys later," Nikki said.

Thirty minutes later, Nikki glanced in the floor-length mirror and could not believe the woman staring back at her. If Corina and the rest of the staff at Bayside could see her now, they would never believe it. Gone were the pumps and dress from earlier in the evening. They were replaced with jeans, a red shirt, brown cowboy boots, and a cowboy hat. Nikki playfully twirled around, looking at herself from the front and back. If she had to say so herself, she looked damn good.

Nikki tilted the hat as she had seen Ross and Junior do a thousand times. She smiled. She wondered what Ross would think of her new attire. She knew he noticed her at supper. Every time their eyes met, her heart turned over a million times. She was not sure what to do about it.

"You look good," Lilly said, coming up behind her. "Look like a real cowgirl."

"Thanks, Lilly. I do clean up good, don't I?"

"Let's get going," Lilly said. "I'm sure the fellas will be wondering where we are."

"Why didn't you tell me that you were coming to dinner tonight?"

"I didn't know I was coming," Lilly said. "Blake called me at the last minute. We've known each other since high school," she said, going into her closet and taking a blue denim jacket off the hanger. "We're good friends, so I went."

"So, there's nothing romantic going on between you two?"

"No. Blake is nice enough but he's a mess."

"Meaning?"

"What I mean is that he's a rich, handsome, and immature boy. He has had everything given to him on a silver spoon. He has no idea what to do with himself. All he thinks about is girls, drinking, and partying. He is gone months at the time with the rodeo. That is not the life for this girl."

"But you came to supper with him?"

"Like I said, we're friends," Lilly said. "I would never date him. Besides, I'm saving up every dollar I can get my hands on. The first chance I get, I am out of here."

Nikki bobbed her head. "Where do you plan on going?"

"I'm not sure." Lilly put on the jacket. "Somewhere on the East Coast. New York. D.C. Anywhere but here."

"I can relate to what you're saying. You sound like me years ago when I left Montgomery."

"Do you regret leaving family and friends?"

"I didn't have many friends because I was considered a geek in school. An outcast. I wore wide-rimmed glasses, had braces, and I was a straight-A student."

Nikki laughed. "Like you said, I was a mess, but my parents were supportive when I decided to attend college so far away from home. I don't regret my decision. It was the best thing that ever happened to me."

Lilly smiled. "You just confirmed for me that I'm doing the right thing. I am going to do it. I am going to go for it."

"What does your family think about you leaving?"

"It's just me," Lilly answered in a sad tone.

"I'm sorry," Nikki said.

"Don't be," Lilly said. "I never knew my father. My mother died two years ago." She dipped her head. "She was killed in a car crash."

Nikki didn't have the words. She reached out and tapped Lilly's hand in comfort.

"It's getting easier," Lilly walked into the small living room and grabbed the car keys out of the ashtray. "So, what is going on between you and Ross?" she asked out of the blue.

Nikki's eyes stretched. "What? Ross? Why would you ask about him?"

"That was some wild, hot primal chemistry going on between you two."

"Don't be ridiculous, Nikki argued. "There is nothing going on between us."

"Keep telling yourself that, you hear. All I know is he couldn't keep his eyes off you all evening, and you avoided eye contact with him, even at supper." She opened the door and walked outside.

"Was it that obvious?" Nikki asked, following Lilly to the car. "Honey, it was clear as glass." Lilly opened the car door and slid behind the wheel. She stuck the key in the ignition. The vehicle purred like a kitten. "If I saw it, I am sure Lena noticed it."

"What about Junior?" Nikki asked.

"He's kind of dense," Lilly said. "I don't know."

Nikki laughed. "He's not dense."

"Come on," Lilly said, pulling out of the driveway. "Junior couldn't find his way out of a paper bag."

* * *

The Big Boot was nothing like Nikki imagined. She thought it would be a loud, dark, smoky hole in the wall with a drunk and disorderly crowd. To her surprise, it was just the opposite. Lilly pulled into the parking lot of a large tan building with a giant neon black-boot sign atop the building. She noticed rows of motorcycles parked next to a water trough. There was a line of people laughing, talking, and cuddling, waiting to get inside. The sounds of country music filled the air.

"Ready?" Lilly said, unbuckling her seatbelt.

"As I'll ever be." Nikki exited the vehicle. She removed her cellphone and quickly snapped a photo of the club. "I'm sending this to my girlfriend in D.C. She will never believe that I went to a cowboy bar. I gotta take a selfie." She chuckled.

A few minutes later, they strolled inside the entrance and walked through a set of swinging saloon doors. Nikki felt as if she stepped back into pages of the Old West. In the center of the floor was a spacious pine dance floor, surrounded by wooden railings with carved round tables behind them. Small lanterns and red-and-white-checkered tablecloths were situated on top. Above the bar was a giant Texas longhorn skull. On the walls, she noticed photos of famous cowboys, including Bill Pickett. There were newspaper clippings of local rodeo top winners, including Ross.

They moved further into the room. There were people everywhere. "Where are they?" Lilly asked, her eyes scanning the room. "They said they would be sitting up front so that we could find them."

Nikki joined Lilly in searching the room. Her eyes were darting to and fro when she heard a deep voice from behind.

"Good evening, ladies."

Nikki's and Lilly's heads turned simultaneously to a tall, slim, young cowboy. He sported a silver belt buckle that read 2010 Rodeo Champ. Her eyes went up and down his body. His dirty-blond hair was cut short to his head. The handsome, rugged, bearded face, with dimples, and blue eyes pulled her in. He smiled, displaying a set of beautiful white teeth. If she were at least ten years younger, he would be her type. D.C. had good-looking men, but she noticed that there was something about Texas men that made her heartbeat speed up.

"Well, if it isn't J.D. Spriggs," Lilly said. "What brings you out to this neck of the woods?"

This was the J.D. Spriggs that was threatening to take the Championship from Ross, Nikki thought to herself. He had to be at least ten years younger that Ross. He was nothing but a kid.

"Aw, you know me." J.D. was nervously spinning the hat in his hands. "Just wanted to venture out." His eyes glanced over to Nikki. "Who is this lovely lady?" He extended a hand.

"Nicole Phillips," she said, accepting his handshake.

"That's Dr. Nicole Phillips to you, J.D.," Lilly chimed in.

J.D. nodded. "I see." A glint appeared in his eyes. "You're the Sawbones everyone is talking about. Their description don't do you justice. You're beautiful." He placed a hand to his chest and coughed. "I'm sick, Doc. Can you help me?"

Nikki rolled her eyes. She heard all the lame doctor jokes over the years. They were getting old. There was something different about J.D. Spriggs. He spoke very articulate. "Where are you from J.D.? I hear an Eastern Accent? New York maybe?"

"The doctor is not only beautiful," J.D. said. "She is very observant. I am from Manhattan."

Nikki leaned back. "Really? Manhattan?"

"What am I doing here, right?"

"Well, yes," Nikki said. "This is hardly the place that I would find a New Yorker. Let alone one riding the rodeo circuit."

J.D. chuckled. "I know, but my family has a second home here in Montgomery. I have been riding for as long as I can remember. I guarantee you that I belong here."

"That is a matter of opinion," Blake said, walking up behind them. He placed an arm around Lilly's waist. Junior, Ross, and Lena brought up the rear.

"Well, if it isn't the Kincaid brothers," J.D. announced. Three young men quickly came and stood beside him.

Nikki could feel the tension level between the men go up one hundred degrees.

"Go suck eggs, J.D.," Blake shouted.

J.D. and his crew laughed.

"Is that all you got, little boy?" J.D. joked.

"Boy? Who are you calling boy? You are only a year older than I am," Blake exclaimed, lunging toward J.D. Ross and Junior held him back.

"Easy now. This is not what we came here for," Ross said in a calm voice. "Take the ladies back to our tables." He turned his back on J.D.

"I'm going to take that title off you at the Sweet Bronco Invitational," J.D. said. "I hope you are cleared to ride."

Ross stopped dead in his tracks. He refocused on J.D. "Why wouldn't I be cleared to ride?"

J.D. walked toward him. The scene was like two gladiators about to do battle. "Word is one bad fall, and you could be in a wheelchair."

Nikki noticed a twitch at Ross's lower jawline. He was doing his best to remain calm. She suddenly thought about his after hour visit to see Dr. Baker. Was it what J.D was referring too?

"I don't know where you heard that rumor," Ross said, "but even if I were in a wheelchair, I can still ride circles around you."

The crowd laughed.

J.D. didn't try to hide his anger. His face clouded. He was embarrassed. "See, that's your problem. You are so damn cocky. Arrogant. I guess I just have to take you down a peg."

"You can try," Ross threw back. "You see, unlike you, I don't have a problem with losing. I welcome it. I have lost before, and I am sure that I will again. But for now, I am the man to beat. If you think you can take that title off me, go for it."

Nikki smiled. He gave a very impressive answer. He was confident. It appears more and more that she may have been wrong about him. She hoped that what J.D. said about his health was not true. She would have to find out from Dr. Baker.

"Like I told you before," Ross said, "just bring your A-game. I have no problem passing the torch."

The onlookers clapped.

"You tell that, young buck," a man shouted.

"Put a hurt on 'em, Ross," another man yelled.

Ross turned around. He came face-to-face with Nikki.

"Well said," Nikki leaned over and whispered.

"I thought so." Ross gestured to lead her to their table.

Nikki walked in front of him, but she could feel his eyes on her every move. A heat wave ran through her body. He pulled out a chair for her next to Lilly and Blake. Junior was nowhere to be found. Lilly nodded and smiled. Blake's eyes picked up on the gesture between the two women. He looked from Nikki to Ross. She dropped her eyes.

"Where's Junior?" Ross asked. He craned his neck around the club.

"He couldn't wait for the waitress and went to get drinks," Blake answered. "He should be back in a moment."

A moment later, a petite, busty brunette dressed in a tight blue tank top, breasts spilling out, came over to the table to take their drink order. "What will it be?"

Nikki was not sure what to order. "I'm not sure. Do you have a menu?"

Everyone at the table laughed except Ross. He surprised her by leaning over and whispering, "No menu."

Nikki was embarrassed. She had to redeem herself. "Then how do first-timers like myself know what to order?"

The waitress was impatient. "Shall I come back?"

"Can you tell me what you have?" Nikki asked.

The waitress looked at her like she lost her mind. "You want me to run down the whole menu?" she quipped.

"It is her first time here," Ross replied.

Lena snapped her fingers. "Waitress, I know what I want."

"She is taking my order," Nikki snapped. She stared at Lena.

"Amy, just bring a pitcher of beer," Ross responded.

"But I wanted to—" Blake began to say. Lilly nudged him in the side, and Ross threw him a look that caused him to back down. "Just what I wanted, beer."

"Me to," Lilly chimed in. "Beer."

"If you guys want anything else just head over to the bar," Ross suggested.

"One pitcher of beer coming up," Amy said and sashayed off.

A few minutes later, Junior reappeared. He was out of breath but a bundle of excitement.

"Don't tell me—you rode the mechanical bull?" Blake said.

"Yep," Junior answered. "Stayed on a whole six seconds," he boasted.

"Stretch must have slowed it down for ya." Blake laughed. "Cuz there's no way you can stay on past three seconds. How much did you pay him?"

"You're a barrel of laughs," Junior said. "Funny."

Everyone at the table looked over at Junior. He looked like the cat that ate the canary. "All right, slipped him a twenty."

Laughter went up around the table.

"I knew it," Ross said. "All those stories you used to tell me about riding the bull in here, they were all lies."

"Yep," Blake teased.

"Not all of them," Junior cried.

Another round of laughter went up around the table.

A moment later, the DJ played "Achy Breaky Heart" by Billy Ray Cyrus. The crowd rushed to the dance floor. Everyone formed a line and began dancing with ease.

Nikki whispered to Junior. "Is that the Texas two-step?"

"No. It's line dancing," Junior answered. "Wanna try it?"

"I don't know," Nikki said. "Like I said earlier, I'm not a good dancer."

"C'mon. It's an easy dance to learn," Junior said. "I'll teach you." He extended a hand to her.

Nikki accepted Juniors' hand. He led her through the crowd to the center of the dance floor. He positioned himself behind her, still holding on to her hand, and began to walk her through the steps. She found herself laughing and moving through the steps. In no time she was line dancing with like a pro.

She glanced over her right shoulder to see Ross and Lena behind them. Next to them was Blake and Lilly. Ross was dancing with ease. For a person with two left feet, he seemed to be having the time of his life. He and Lena appear close. She felt a twinge of jealousy when he smiled at Lena.

"See, you got it," Junior was saying. "You're a natural. A quick study."

"Only because you are here."

The music slowed down. Junior held out his hands, asking permission to take her in his arms. She glanced out of the corner of her eye to see Ross and Lena dancing close. "Why not," she managed to say.

Junior wrapped his arms around her waist, pulling her close. His hands moved down to the small of her back. She rested her head in his chest. They began dancing slow, in sync with the music. She closed her eyes. She had two left feet, but right now, it felt good to be in his arms.

"Are you enjoying yourself?" Junior asked in a low, sultry tone.

Nikki looked up in his face. His eyes locked with hers. His breathing was a little ragged. She could tell he was trying his best to compose himself, but the bulge between them told a different story; he had lost the battle. "Not as good as you are," she joked.

Junior chuckled. "I can't help it, dancing with a beautiful woman in my arms makes my temperature go through the roof."

"I understand," Nikki said. "But just so you know, your cowboy boots won't be under my bed come morning."

"Okay!" Junior exclaimed. He playfully twirled her around. "Now did this good ole cowboy give any hints that I am after your goods?"

Nikki fell into his chest again. "Just making sure there are no misunderstandings."

"Is it because we just met?"

"Of course."

Junior smiled down at her." I can respect that. But just so that you know, this old boy doesn't give up that easy."

Nikki and Junior danced a couple more songs. The music sped up. She broke out some old, rusty moves that she remembered. She didn't care how foolish she looked. She was having fun.

* * *

Thirty minutes later, Junior escorted her to her seat. She looked to see Blake and Lilly headed toward the table. They were in a heated argument. "What's the matter?" Nikki inquired.

"This fool wants to ride the bull."

"What is wrong with that?" Junior asked.

"You know what happened the last time you got on that thing," Lilly explained. "Your arm was in a cast for weeks."

"That's child play compared to what can happen in a real rodeo," Junior said. "He's a big boy. Let him ride." He focused on Nikki. "If anything happens we have a doctor that can fix him up."

"He's drunk," Lilly said. "The last thing he needs is for you egging him on."

"You don't think I can ride," Blake cried. "I'll show you." He pushed his way through the crowd.

Nikki looked to see J.D. within earshot. He winked and tilted the brim of his hat at her. "Junior, stop him. He's in no condition to ride."

Junior ignored her pleas. "He'll be fine."

Folks made their way up front to get a view or hung on the outside of the railing. The youngest Kincaid hopped on the bull from the rear. He sat on the saddle. He gripped the ropes and got into his stance. He nodded to Stretch. The bull began moving slow at first. Nikki was fascinated at the event.

The speed increased. The bull began thrashing wildly. Blake was still in control. The crowd was clapping and jeering him on. Junior had a large grin on his face. Lilly was frantic and disappeared in the crowd.

Nikki looked back in time to see Blake landing with a thud. She rushed to his side. He lay motionless for a moment. "Blake, can you hear me. Are you alright? Are you hurt anywhere?"

"I'm fine." He winced. "I just got the wind knocked out of me. Damn bull. I came close," he said, getting to his feet. "Big brother is going to give me the speech."

"He should," Nikki cried. "That was stupid. You could have been injured."

"Not you too," Blake whined. "I am a big boy. I can take care of myself."

Almost on cue, Ross appeared out of the crowd. "Are you crazy?"

"Yes, he is," Lilly agreed. "He needs to have his head examined."

"You went to get my big brother," Blake replied. "I don't believe this."

"Nikki, how is he?" Ross asked.

"He seems to be fine," Nikki said, trying to diffuse the situation. "If you want I can check him out at the clinic."

"That offer still stands to check me out, Doc," J.D. said, stepping up next for the bull.

"Give it a rest, J.D.," Ross said. "No one here is taking the bait."

J.D. smirked. "Fine." He jumped on the bull. "Let me show you how it's done and why I will become the next champion."

Ross was not intimidated. He stepped back from in front of the bull. He spread his arms apart. "Have at it," he said and vanished as fast as he came.

Nikki watched Ross strut with his head held high. "The man gets some cool points for handling himself like a man tonight," she said to herself.

Chapter Seven

"So, you're not going to do anything?" David asked as he and Winston were sitting in a booth at Cadence Supper Club. For the past couple of days, he had been meeting with anyone on the hospital board who would listen to try and reinstate Nikki. "She was one of the hospital's best surgeons, not to mention your ex-fiancée."

"She's also someone who took a bat to my car," Winston said.

"Can you blame her?"

"Whose side are you on?"

"I'm not on anyone's side," David answered. "I'm just saying that I can understand why she did what she did. She lost it, but that's no reason to have a black mark on her stellar career as a physician."

Winston looked down at the bottom of his glass as if he would find the answer there. "I will think about what you said. But I can't promise anything."

David shook his head in disbelief. "You're all heart, do you know that?"

"Yeah, I know I'm a real bastard."

"When did you become like this?"

"How do you know I wasn't always like this?" Winston said. "Huh?" He tapped David on the back.

"No. You weren't always like this," David replied. "Cold. Uncaring. I remember a different person in medical school. This isn't you. What you did to Nikki, definitely isn't the man I know. What you did was low, even for you."

Winston's face clouded. "That's enough."

"It was bad enough that you cheated on her, married someone else, but then you stuck the knife in deeper by getting her fired."

"Nikki will be fine. She is an excellent surgeon. She can get a job anywhere."

"Just not at Bayside," David replied with sarcasm.

Winston sighed. "Look, if you like, I can make some calls and see about getting her on at another hospital. I have friends over at St. Charles."

David threw a couple of crumpled-up bills on the table. "Don't bother; Nikki already found something."

Winston leaned back in the chair.

"What? You look surprised," David said. "Didn't you just say that she could get work anywhere? She did find another job."

"How do you know?"

"Does it matter?" David asked.

"Where did she get on?" Winston asked. "Is it a local hospital?"

"Why do you care?" David said. "But if you must know it's a private clinic on the outside of Houston, Texas," he answered, and walked away. "Bastard," he muttered under his breath.

* * *

"David, I'm sorry for the way I acted and the things that I said to you," Nikki said the next morning at the clinic. David had called her by video chat. She arrived a couple of hours early. Junior promised to teach her to ride and give her a tour of the ranch. She was on her way to the barn when he phoned. "I had no right to blame you." She looked up to see the most beautiful sunrise that she'd ever seen. The orange, blue, and yellow skyline was breathtaking. For the first time in her life, she was learning to appreciate sunrises, morning dew on the grass, and fresh air so clean that you could sink your teeth into it. It was amazing.

"I'm going to get your job back if it's the last thing that I do."

"David, I think it's wonderful what you are trying to do, but don't worry about me."

"Excuse me, but is sounds like you don't want to come back," David said. "What's going on?"

"Nothing is going on," Nikki said. She continued looking at the sunrise. "I'm just seeing a lot of things for the first time, that's all."

"Does this have anything to do with a certain cowboy that Corina was telling me about?"

"This has nothing to do with a cowboy," Nikki said. "It's just me finding myself for the first time, that's all."

A knock on the door caused David to look up. Corina stuck her head around the door. He waved her inside. "I'm on video chat with Nikki."

Corina sauntered further into the room. She looked over David's shoulder. "You guys made up?"

"It was just a misunderstanding," David said.

Corina smiled and waved. "Hey gurl."

Nikki's face lit up at seeing her friend. "Corina, how are you?"

"Working hard as usual."

"She's lying," David replied. "If she were, she wouldn't be in my office."

"I came to ask if he was interested in going to the RFK Ranch with me," Corina said. "I was hoping that you two would make up but, he beat me to it."

"What?" Nikki exclaimed. "Are you serious? You're coming here?"

"Well, it's time for the annual family vacation. I'm tired of seeing Mickey Mouse. I was talking to my husband about doing something a little different this year."

"And?" Nikki prompted.

"He loved the idea of going to a dude ranch."

Nikki squealed. "You guys will love it. The kids will get a chance to ride horses, camp out, and hang out with real cowboys. It's the vacation of all vacations."

"You don't have to sell me. I like the idea," Corina said.

"Sounds like someone else likes it there," David said.

"It's beautiful here."

"Hmmm," Corina teased. "How's Ross?"

"Ross? Who's Ross?" David asked in a curious tone. "Is he the cowboy Corina was talking about?"

"He's Winston's replacement." Corina chuckled.

"Really?" David said, amused. "This is huge."

"Corina, will you stop?" Nikki pleaded. "Let me know when you book the reservation."

"It will be before you complete your community service," Corina said. "Maybe you can get us the family plan."

"Consider it done."

"Wait. What community service?" David asked. "No one tells me anything. Why haven't I heard about this?"

"I will fill you in later," Corina said.

"Good morning, Nikki," Ross said, breaking into her conversation.

Nikki turned around. She was at a loss for words upon seeing him. She didn't think that he could look more handsome than he had last night, but she was wrong. The handsome cowboy. The beautiful sunrise. Both were the perfect setting for a romantic moment.

Her eyes took in the full sight of him from head to toe. "Ross," she said in a low tone. "Good morning. How are you?"

"I'm great," Ross said. "Thanks for asking."

"You're up early. Where are you headed?" Nikki could have kicked herself. It was a stupid question, but she couldn't think of anything else to say to him. When they were at each other throats, she had plenty to say. Now, whenever she lay eyes on him, her brain turns to mush.

"I've been up for several hours."

"Dr. Baker told me that you guys get up pretty early around here." Nikki said. "He wasn't lying."

"We get up before the cock's crow. I had to break a stallion," he explained.

"I wish I could have seen you in action," Nikki said. "I'm told you're one of the best in the state."

Ross flashed that smile of his. This time, it was welcomed. "I am the best in the country," he bragged.

"Excuse me," Nikki replied. "Aren't we modest? Bragging."

"It ain't bragging if it's true." He lifted his head and looked at the morning skyline.

Nikki's eyes followed his. "It's lovely, isn't it? You're so lucky to have grown up here."

"I know," Ross said. "There is no other place I'd rather be."

"From what I have seen, I can understand," Nikki said. "This is my first time on a ranch. I have to tell you, I'm fascinated by it all."

"You grew up in Montgomery, but you've never been on a ranch?" Ross asked.

"Have you been to Montgomery?"

"I've only passed through," Ross said. "It's a nice little town."

"Then you know it's not a cowboy town."

Ross half-smiled. He shrugged. "I have to agree with you there, it wasn't much to see."

"Not even close," Nikki said, looking around for Junior. "Have you seen your brother this morning?" She glanced at her watch. "He was supposed to give me a tour of the ranch. Give me a riding lesson."

"He's going to be tied up for a while," Ross answered. "If you can stand to be in my company, I could show you around the resort. Give you a quick lesson."

"Sure," Nikki said.

"Let's meet in front of the manor in about ten minutes," Ross said.

"I'll be there," Nikki said as she watched him walk away. He looked as good going as he did coming. She licked her lips.

"Nothing going on, huh?" Corina said, breaking into her thoughts.

"Oh my God," Nikki exclaimed. She completely forgot that she was in a video chat with David and Corina. They overheard everything. She wanted to slink away.

"I told you, David," Corina teased. "Ross sounds dreamy. Sexy, deep voice. He likes you. I can tell."

"C'mon, he's just showing me around the ranch, that's all."

"Right," Corina replied. "What do you think, David?"

"He likes her. She likes him," David said. "But I never figured you for the cowboy type. I can't imagine seeing you on a horse. You are too prissy for that."

"You would be surprised what you find out about yourself," Nikki said.

"Is he a real cowboy?" David asked. "You know, riding, bronco busting, roping, and all that stuff we see on television."

"Ross has been the national rodeo champion for the past three years."

"What? Are you kidding me?" Corina exclaimed. "Ross is the real thing."

"Yes, he is," Nikki bragged. "He does it all."

"I have to meet this guy," David said. "I think I'm having a man crush."

They laughed.

"Look, guys, I have to go," Nikki said. "It's not good to keep a cowboy waiting."

They said their goodbyes. Nikki found herself anxious to see Ross again. She rushed over to meet him in front of the manor.

Ross appeared a few minutes later. Gone were the vest, gloves, and chaps. She was a little disappointed. But he still looked delicious. He stopped in front of her. A heat wave washed over her.

"What would you like to see first?" Ross inquired.

"You're the tour guide," Nikki said.

"You can't ride?"

"Not even a little bit."

"I'll tell you what, I will give you a tour first. Then, I'll teach you how to ride," Ross replied. "Just the basics."

"Enough to where I won't fall off."

Ross threw his head back and laughed. She liked the sound of his laugh. The way his brown eyes sparkled when he smiled was infectious. It was adorable. You cannot help but join in his laughter.

"It's good to see you laugh," Nikki said out loud. "You should do it more often."

Ross's eyes locked with hers. "You think so?"

"I do," Nikki said. "It's better than that mean grouch always walking around in a bad mood."

"Tell me what you really think."

"I'm just being honest."

Ross took her to the resort. He introduced her to the front desk staff. They left the main lobby and headed next door to the log cabins. Guests could choose to live inside for their stay or sleep out amongst the stars in a tent under the Texas sky. He took her inside one of the empty rooms. It was decorated with a gas fireplace and full bath. It was comfortable.

After they left the cabin, Ross took her over to meet some of the ranch hands. They were getting ready to cut some steers. She found out many of the workers not only worked at the ranch and resort but also competed on the rodeo circuit. They were also responsible for taking the guests on the trail rides, fly-fishing, on hikes, and on a real-life Western experience in a horse-drawn stagecoach.

Ross talked her into going to a riding demonstration.

Since she was unable to ride a horse, she rode on a wagon with some of the other guests. She watched with interest as Ross rode on what was called cutting horses, where they singled out a steer from the herd. Afterward, wranglers took over to take care of the rest of the group.

"That was amazing," Nikki exclaimed a couple of hours later as they walked back toward the resort. "To witness it in person is on a whole other level, and the men were so sweet."

"I think it's you," Ross said. "I know those guys. Sweet is not the word I'd use to describe that bunch."

"I may have some business for the resort. My friend, Corina, and her family decided not to see Mickey Mouse this year and will be coming here instead."

"We were chosen over Disneyland," Ross said. "I don't believe it."

"Well, believe it," Nikki said. "She has two boys, ages seven and eleven. I know they will get a kick out of this place. They will love the horses."

"We have thousands for them to choose from."

"Thousands?"

"RFK has the finest stock and breed in the country," Ross explained. "It's one of the things that sets us apart from other ranches. People come here to relax, enjoy themselves, and leave whatever is bothering them behind. We try to give them a real Western experience. It's one of the reason we don't have TVs or computers in the rooms. We take them out on the trail or the mountains. There is no reception for phones and whatnots. It is just you and Mother Nature. The world of technology is shut out."

"How do you stand it?" Nikki said. "No phone. I don't know what I'd do without my phone. I guess it's from being on call all of the time, and I'm used to having it with me. But I admit since I have been here, I haven't had much need for it."

"Trust me, once you get out on the open range, you don't miss things like modern technology."

Nikki tucked a strand of hair behind her ear. "I envy you. Everything is simple for you. You like being a cowboy."

"I was born a cowboy. It's certain I will die one," Ross replied. "It's the same for you, I suspect, with what you do. You're a doctor. You enjoy what you do."

"I do."

"Did you always want to be a doctor?"

"For as long as I can remember," Nikki said. "I remember when I was a little girl, I used to bring home small wounded animals, like birds, dogs, and rabbits. I drove my parents crazy."

"Look at you now," Ross said.

"Yeah, well, I worked my butt off to get to medical school, graduate second in my class, and then prove myself as an equal among the men in my field. It wasn't easy, but I did it."

Ross nodded his head. "Yes. You did it. Why did you choose orthopedic?"

Nikki wondered if she should tell Ross that it was because of Winston that she chose the specialty. "A friend of mine suggested it. I wasn't sure at first that it was right for me, but I can honestly say that I like it."

"And lucrative," Ross tossed in.

"Not as lucrative as your professions," Nikki replied. "Who would ever think that riding a horse is worth millions."

"Only if you are the champion," Ross reminded her as they walked out one of the side doors of the resort. He led her out onto one of the trails. "I admire you."

"I respect what you do." Nikki looked up. "I didn't get that memo, because when we first met, you were so mean to me."

Ross plucked a honeysuckle, placed it in his mouth, and began chewing on it. "You're right. When we first met, I wasn't nice to you and—"

"You had me arrested!" Nikki exclaimed. "I never even had a parking ticket. Never been in trouble with the law and you had me arrested."

"I'm sorry about that."

"Then you set me up to work here to pay off my debt."

"And you hate it?"

The question caught Nikki off guard. "I wouldn't say hate," she said. "It just wasn't in my plans."

"It's beginning to grow on ya."

"Maybe," she said, being coy.

"I see, don't want to admit it."

"It's not that."

"Tell me about Dr. Nicole Phillips."

"What is there to say?" she asked.

"What about a beau?"

Nikki lowered her eyes. She slowed her pace.

Ross looked behind him. "What's wrong? Did I ask a personal question?"

"No. It's okay."

"You don't have to tell me," Ross said. "It really is none of my business."

Nikki grabbed a blade of grass. "My ex-fiancé dumped me and married another woman," she explained in a rush of breath.

Ross whistled. "I didn't see that coming. I knew something was eating at ya, but I never expected to hear this. Is that why you left town?"

"Let's say I was run out of town," Nikki said. "His new wife's father is on the hospital's board of directors, and they voted to have me fired."

Ross frowned. "Just because your ex-boyfriend married the daughter. How can they do that?"

"Well, that's not all to it," Nikki said in a small, nervous tone.

Ross gave her a suspicious look. "What did you do?"

She shuffled from one foot to the other. "I took a baseball bat to his Mercedes. I broke out all of the windows."

To her surprised, Ross threw his head back and laughed. "Remind me never to get on your bad side." He pointed at her. "I was right; you are a little spitfire. That's something the women around here would do. Good for you."

She shrugged. "I'm out of a job because of it."

"I'm sure you will find something better. I wouldn't fret about it."

"I can't believe I told you. I haven't told anyone."

"Not even Junior." Ross said.

"No."

"You know Junior has a thing for you."

Nikki lazily tilted her head to one side. "Junior is nice."

"But?" Ross prompted.

"But nothing," Nikki answered. "He's nice, but I don't see him in that way."

"What way is that?" Ross inquired, smiling at her with his eyes.

Nikki knew what Ross was trying to insinuate. "Having fun?"

"'Bout as much as I did last night, doing that line dance."

Nikki punched him in the arm. "Are you joking? You were good. You were on rhythm and everything. I was surprised. I thought you had two left feet; I was wrong."

"I've been known to cut a rug or two in my day, but I'm not a fan of that dance," Ross replied. "But on a serious note, I want to thank you for looking after Blake last night."

"No need to thank me," Nikki said. "I was just doing my job."

"Yeah, well, your job is at the Gallop Clinic and not at some dance hall."

"My job is wherever I find it, and last night it just so happened to be at The Big Boot."

She stole a glance at Ross as they came upon an apple tree next to a pond. He sat down with his back to the bark of the tree. He removed his hat and crossed his ankles. He patted the area next to him.

"Have a seat, Sawbones."

Nikki dropped down next to Ross. "Sawbones?"

"Yeah, it means doctor."

"I know what it means," Nikki said. "It's just when I hear it I think of some old man."

"Like Dr. Baker. Trust me; no one would ever get you two mixed up."

"Glad to hear it."

Ross leaned his head back and closed his eyes. Nikki cleared her throat.

Ross's eyes popped open. "What's on your mind?"

"I just wanted to commend you on how you handled the situation with J.D. He was provoking you. You were so cool. Calm. You didn't let him get under your skin, unlike me."

Ross leaned forward. "Completely different situation. You were emotionally involved with your ex. You trusted him. He betrayed you. If I were in the same situation, I might have done the same thing. J.D. is just a young tenderfoot that is on my heels. No worries."

"He seems to think that he will beat you and take the title."

"Not in Houston he won't," Ross said with confidence.

"I like your confidence." She wondered how she could bring up the injury J.D. had alluded to. She figured Ross was a proud man; she knew that about him. He would never voluntarily talk about it. She had to be careful. "I saw you at the clinic yesterday. Is there anything wrong?"

Ross smirked. "I know you heard what J.D. said. What do you want to know?"

"Will you tell me?"

"Why? All you have to do is look at my records," Ross answered. "They will tell you everything you want to know."

Nikki arched an eyebrow. "I want to hear it from you."

"I have nothing to say, except I won't quit competing until I am dethroned or I am no longer able to ride."

"I thought as much. What does Lena think about it?"

Ross threw her a look. He chuckled. "Is that your way of finding out if there is something going on between us?"

"I wasn't very subtle," Nikki said. "Being a doctor, I'm not good at subtlety."

Ross reached out and touched her hand. It was warm to the touch; it was a small gesture, but it felt good.

"That's one of the things I like about you."

"I thought you said I had to be taught a lesson," she teased.

"I just meant I had to take you down a peg," he teased.

"But to answer your question, Lena is like a little sister to me. We have been friends for many years. I don't want to hurt her."

"You have to tell her the truth," Nikki said. "You just have to handle her with kid gloves."

"I know," Ross replied. "Enough about Lena. How about going for a ride?" He pulled her to her feet. "Let's head over to the stables. We have a horse by the name of Sugar that you will fall in love with."

"Sugar?"

"She's a sweet, gentle horse. Some horses like carrots, but she likes cubes of sugar as a treat."

"This is a first," Nikki said. She followed Ross down to the stables and inside the stall of a palomino. She reached out and touched the mane. "It's beautiful."

"His name is Chuckles," Ross explained.

"Chuckles?" she repeated. "Why Chuckles?"

"He's always laughing."

"How can you tell?" Nikki asked.

"If you have been around horses for as long as I have, you learned to recognize the moods," Ross explained. He headed over into Sugar's stall, the spurs on his boots jingling as he moved about. "They are just like people. In so many ways," he said. "They feel things just like we do. Don't you, gurl." He grabbed a red blanket and placed it on her back, gently speaking to and touching her as he prepared her for the ride. "This is Sugar."

Nikki watched as he genuinely took care of the horse. He was so gentle. She could tell that he cared about the horse.

"Ready to head out?" Ross said, grabbing Sugar by the reins and leading her out of the stables.

"I'm looking forward to the riding lesson," Nikki said.

"Me too," Ross answered. "Hold on a second." He disappeared inside the stables.

"There you are," Junior said, rushing toward Nikki in a hurry. "I've been looking all over for you."

"Junior," Nikki exclaimed. She craned her neck, searching for Ross. "Uh, where were you? I waited for you. When you did not show, I—"

"I'm sorry. I got held up with work." Junior looked over and spotted Sugar. "Who took Sugar out?"

"I did," Ross said, coming up behind them with Bullet.

His eyes fell on Nikki. "I was going to give the doctor a quick lesson, but now that you're here I can get to my other chores."

Nikki gave Ross an inquisitive look to see if he was disappointed by what had just happened. If he was, he didn't show it. He grabbed Bullet's reins and mounted the horse.

"Thanks for looking after Nikki."

Nikki's heart sank. Ross tipped his hat. She watched as he rode down the trail. His shoulders appeared to be a little lower than they had been earlier. A moment later, Lena rode out to meet him. They both dismounted from their horses. Lena stuck her arm through his and they walked off together. Her breath caught in her chest. She turned to find Junior watching her.

"Let's go," he said, trying to put her feet in the stirrup. She fell hard on her bottom.

She sat in the dirt for a moment. Not only was she not with the man she wanted to be with, but she was also embarrassed. She wondered how she always found herself in these predicaments.

Chapter Eight

"I had a good time last night," Lena said. She looked at Ross. It appeared as if he was in another world. She snapped her fingers. "Earth to Ross."

"I'm sorry. What did you say?"

"I was talking about last night, I had a really good time."

"Me too."

"I was thinking we should do it again, but next time just the two of us," Lena suggested.

"I'll think about it," Ross said in a casual tone.

"Ross, what's on your mind?"

"Just thinking about the Invitational."

"Nothing to worry about. You have it locked like you always do." Lena stood in front of him. "Are you sure there's nothing else bothering you?"

Ross looked directly in her face. "Like?"

"I met Junior on the way over here. We saw you and the doctor together."

"What of it?" Ross asked in a flat tone. "I was going to teach her to ride because Junior was tied up. But he showed up; he is teaching her, and that's all there is to it."

"As long as that's all it is. Are ready for the Invitational?" she asked, changing the subject.

"Stupid question. I'm always ready."

Lena stopped in her tracks. Her face became serious. "What about your injury?"

"What about it?"

Lena playfully pushed him "Ross Kincaid, you are the stubbornest man I have ever met. Are you serious? What do you mean, what about it?"

"No need to worry about me," Ross said in an irritated tone.

"Every time you get on that bull you are taking a chance," Lena fused. "I'm scared out of my mind."

"I wish folks would quit talking about my injury," Ross stomped inside the manor.

Lena followed. "Ross, everyone is concerned about you, that's all."

"I know that." Ross said. "But I'm sick and tired of folks bringing it up all of the times. Give me some credit, I know what I am doing."

"I'm sorry, Ross." Lena followed him into the kitchen. She watched as he opened and slammed the kitchen cabinet doors. She has never seen him like this before. He was irritated. He was always kind and soft-spoken with her.

On the way over to the ranch this morning, Lena ran into Junior. They walked over to the stables together. Both stood on the hill and watched as Ross and Nikki laughed, talked, and flirted with each other.

He was interested in her; there was no doubt about it. For the first time since Hailey left, Ross was showing interest in another woman, and it wasn't her.

"What are you looking for?"

Ross moved over to the refrigerator. He opened the water department door and removed a bottle. "Found it."

"You have been in a huff since Junior ruined your plans with the doctor."

Ross hand stopped in mid-motion. "Lena, stop it. Please don't make a big deal out of this."

Lena crossed her arms across her chest. "I'm not making a big deal out of it. You two looked mighty cozy with each other."

Ross almost choked on the water. "No, we didn't."

"Junior also saw it," Lena replied.

"Which is why I saddled Sugar," Ross replied. "I didn't want him to get the wrong understanding."

"You were just being polite."

"If that's what you want to call it." Ross turned on his heels and strolled out of the kitchen. "I'd better get going. I have lots of work to do around here." He hurried out the door and walked into the barn. He headed to the back of the barn to check on the machines milking the cows. "I just lied," he said aloud. "I'm interested in Nikki. Very interested. God, I don't want to hurt my brother." He paced up and down the aisle as if he were telling his problem to the animals. "Family comes first."

"Who are you talking to?" a shirtless Blake asked, coming from the back of the barn.

Ross was startled. He quickly recovered. "Nobody," he said, and stormed toward the front.

Blake was hot on his trail. "I heard you. You are interested in someone, and I believe I know who."

Ross ignored him. He hurried in the room with the mechanical bull

Blake snapped his fingers. "I know. You discovered that you have feelings for Lena."

Ross didn't respond. He hurried over and put on a pair of riding gloves.

"Come on, big brother, talk to me," Blake pleaded. "This is important."

"So is winning the Invitational, which I have to get ready for. Time me or get out. I need to concentrate."

Blake blinked. "I'll time you." He opened a drawer and removed a stopwatch.

Ross jumped on the mechanical bull like a professional. He grabbed the reins, took his stance, and nodded to Blake.

Blake took a deep breath and pushed the button.

The mechanical bull began to buck and twist. Ross was able to hold on for four seconds before being thrown. He landed on the hay-covered floor with a thud. Blake rushed to his side, a look of concern on his face.

"Ross, all you all right?"

Ross managed to stand to his feet. He brushed the hay off. "Damn it; I can stay on longer than that," he exclaimed.

"Usually, you can," Blake said. "You seem distracted."

"Just a little," Ross admitted. He placed his hands on his hips and began pacing the floor, looking at the bull. He imagined himself in the stall at the Invitational just before the bull was released. He collected his thoughts. Controlled his breathing. His focus was on nothing but the eight seconds he would need to walk away with the win. He clasped his hands together, he hopped back on the bull, and positioned himself. "Let's do this."

* * *

Nikki accepted Juniors' hand to help her from the horse. Her bottom was sore. Her entire body was aching from head to toe.

"You did well," Junior said.

"Are you joking? My entire body is killing me." Nikki began stretching. "It's been a week. I haven't learned a thing."

"That's not true," Junior said in a soft tone. He grabbed Sugar by the reins and led her to the pond.

Nikki noticed that Junior seemed a little distant. During the ride, he was pleasant enough, but he was not his usual self. She grabbed Chuckle's reins and stood beside him. "What is it, Junior? What's wrong?"

Junior kneeled down. He picked up a pebble and skipped it on the water. "What do you mean?"

"I mean you weren't your usual perky self. What's wrong?"

"You're the doctor," Junior reminded her. "You tell me."

"I am an orthopedist. I am not a Psychiatrist."

Junior let out a nervous cough. "I don't know how to say it."

"You just open your mouth and say it."

"Okay. I have never met a woman like you before. I have never felt this way about anyone."

Nikki leaned back. She knew that Junior liked her. She enjoyed his company. But to hear him pour his heart out like this was a surprise. Junior was a good man. She didn't want to hurt his feelings, but she didn't feel the same way about him.

"Junior I—" Nikki began to say.

"Let me finish," Junior continued. "It took a lot of courage for me to get up the nerve to say this to you."

"Junior just—"

"Quiet, woman," Junior said. "You don't know when to shut up. When a man is pouring his heart to you, that is the time to remain silent."

Nikki's eyes stretched. "Excuse me. You got the floor."

"Thank you," Junior continued. "As I was saying, since that day you crashed into our fence, I've been attracted to you. You are beautiful, intelligent, and full of fire. You are one hell of a woman."

"A hell of a woman? You couldn't think of anything better to say than that?"

"Will you let me finish?"

"Okay. Okay," Nikki replied. "I'm sorry."

"This week has been the best time that I have had in a long time. I have become even more attracted to you. I was thinking that I would like for us to be more than friends. Maybe, I can come to Montgomery to see you."

"Junior." Nikki shook her head. "I don't know. I mean, I—"

"Like my brother," Junior finished for her.

Nikki rocked in her boots "What? What are you talking about?"

Junior placed a gloved hand to his head. "Why is it always him?"

Nikki arched a perfect arched eyebrow. "Him who?"

"Ross. Don't think that I haven't noticed the way you look at him."

"That's not true," Nikki argued. "Isn't it?"

"I have seen the two of you together," Junior said. "Smiling and flirting with each other. Lena saw it, too."

"Junior, it was innocent. Ross was just showing me around because you were late. You really are making a big deal out of nothing. Besides, I have been spending all of my time with you."

"That is true."

"If you think that I like your brother, then why are you spending time with me?"

"I told you, because I like you," Junior replied.

"I take offense to what you are implying." Nikki tried to look hurt. Junior gave her an inquisitive look. She looked away. She began petting Chuckles to calm her nerves.

"I'm sorry, Nikki. I didn't mean to offend you," Junior said. "It's just that I feel that we have something going on between us. The way you look at him reminded me of another incident involving another woman."

Nikki's interest was piqued. "Another incident?"

"It happened a long time ago," Junior answered. He grabbed Sugar's reins. "Let's head back. You need to get to the clinic. I'm sure Dr. Baker is wondering where you are."

As they headed back, Nikki wondered if the other incident was Hailey, Ross's ex-fiancée.

* * *

"Nikki can get us a great deal," Corina said to her husband, Oscar, on the phone. She was doing her best to convince him that going to a ranch resort would be more entertaining not only for the kids but for her as well. She missed Nikki. The orthopedic department was not the same without her best friend. "It will be fantastic for the kids. Plus, if I see Mickey Mouse once more, I'm going to scream."

"The kids like Disneyland," Oscar replied.

"They can see Mickey again next year, but this year we are doing something different. We are doing something for the adults."

"It seems you have already made up your mind," Oscar said. "Just tell me the plans like you always do."

"We are not going to Disneyland," Corina said. "You can't tell me that being a cowboy doesn't interest you."

"Well, now that I think about it," Oscar admitted. "I cannot wait to get out on the range."

"I feel the same. The boys are going to love it." The door to her office opened. She looked up to see Winston sauntering in. He grabbed a magazine off the stand. She frowned. *What does he want?* she thought to herself. "I'll call and make the reservation." She ended the call.

Winston sat in the chair across from her desk. He casually flipped through the pages.

Corina leaned back in her chair. "Dr. Thorpe. What can I do for you?"

"Things are slow. I was out and about. I wanted to see how you were doing." He stood and walked over to the bookcase and began playing with a toy helicopter. He spotted a candy bowl and grabbed a strawberry lollipop.

Corina looked at Winston with disdain. She knew him well enough to know when he wanted something. This was not an ordinary visit.

Winston removed the plastic wrapping and placed the candy in his mouth. "I heard through the grapevine that Nikki works at some rodeo clinic. Is it true?"

"Why do you want to know?"

"I'm just curious." Winston smirked. "I mean, with all of her experience, she couldn't find a better job than at some small clinic."

"With all due respect, Dr. Thorpe, I am not going to discuss Nikki with you."

Winston sighed. "You never liked me, did you?"

"I liked you fine until you hurt my friend," Corina said. "Then you had a great doctor fired because you didn't have the balls to face up to what you did."

Winston shoved his hands in his white lab coat pockets. "How you feel about me shouldn't have anything to do with you answering my questions."

"If I don't answer, are you going to have me fired, too?"

Winston didn't respond. He looked as if he wanted to say something but thought better of it. Instead he turned and walked out the way he came in.

* * *

"I've decided to come with you," David announced the next day as he fell into step with Corina in the hospital hallway. "I found that I need a nice, long vacation from this place. I'm beginning to think that it was a good idea that Nikki left when she did."

"I know what you mean. Have you heard the latest rumor?"

"What is it?"

"That Nikki tried to attack Winston's new wife before she left."

"Ridiculous," David said. "I wouldn't be surprised if Winston didn't spread it himself."

"You think he would?" Corina asked, glancing over at David. "I put nothing past Winston these days," David said. "I did hear that the Orthopedic clinic is getting another doctor to take her place."

"She hasn't been gone two weeks and they're already making plans to replace her," Corina said.

"Well, in their defense," David said as he followed her in the clinic, "they do need someone to take over her patients full-time."

"I miss Nikki," Corina said as they stood in front of the receptionist desk. "When I last spoke to her, she sounded pleasant enough, but you could tell that she was down."

"You spoke with Dr. Phillips?" Chloe asked. "How is she doing?"

Several nurses stopped in mid-motion when they heard Nikki's name.

"Nikki is doing great," David answered for Corina. "She is working at the Gallop Clinic on the RFK Dude ranch."

"It's filled with handsome cowboys," Corina chimed in as Winston came within earshot.

"She always was lucky like that," one of the nurses joked.

"That is right outside of Houston," a male patient on crutches said, hobbling up to the desk. "I know that ranch. It's owned by the Kincaid's."

"You know them?" Corina asked.

He half-smiled. "I don't know them personally, but they are a very wealthy African-American family. The RFK Ranch has been in existence for generations. Franklin Kincaid Sr. started the Gallop Clinic after he was injured from a rodeo fall. It's also a very successful resort. A friend of mine on the rodeo circuit was treated there. It's very reputable. Good doctors. If Dr. Phillips is there, I'll drop in the next time I'm in Houston, and say hello."

"He's right," David said. "I did research on the Gallop Clinic. Small but very high tech."

Winston strolled over and stood next to David. "Why didn't you tell me Nikki was working on a ranch?"

"You know the answer to that," David said. He refocused on the male patient. "What do you know about Ross Kincaid?"

Corina's eyes lit up. "Yeah, do you know anything about him?"

"Bad-ass national rodeo champion for the past three years or so," he said. "I had the chance to see him compete a couple of times. He puts on a good show. He's the best in the business."

Corina smiled. "I can't wait to meet him."

"Why?" Chloe asked.

Corina glanced over at Winston. "He and Nikki are seeing each other."

Chloe's mouth gaped. "Dr. Phillips is dating a cowboy?"

"You heard it here first," Corina said.

"I have to Google him," Chloe said. She quickly typed in *Cowboy Ross Kincaid.* His picture and profile instantly popped on the screen. "Talk about good looking."

"Let me see," one of the nurses exclaimed. "He's handsome."

The other staff members huddled around the screen. "I'll like to ride him," another nurse exclaimed. "That brother is fine!"

"He can rope me any time," another one said.

"I can honestly say I am looking forward to meeting him for a different reason," David said. "I'm looking forward to trying my hand at roping, riding, barrel racing, and maybe spending a night out on the range under the stars."

"That sounds so romantic," Chloe said. "I wish I could go."

"Don't worry, I will take lots of pictures," Corina teased.

Winston gave David and Corina a hard look before storming off down the hall.

The rest of the staff members burst out laughing. "Do you think he's jealous?" David asked.

"I think so," Chloe answered. "Did you see that trail of dust that he left behind?"

"Serves him right," Corina echoed.

* * *

The next morning, Ross woke up in pain. His lower back felt as if it were on fire. He was thrown again in practice yesterday, now he was paying for it. He tried to sit up but was unable to move. He knew what was wrong. The sciatic nerve in his back had flared up again. He experienced it several times before, whenever he overdid it. All he needed was to get in contact with Dr. Baker and receive a steroid epidural shot. He would be fine.

His mind went to Nikki. He hadn't seen or spoken to her since the morning he had given her a tour of the ranch. He convinced himself that not seeing her was best for both of them. The fate of his relationship with Junior depended on it. He had never known his brother to be so taken with a woman before. He hadn't been attracted to anyone since Hailey. She would be gone in a couple of days. Everything will be fine.

Ross could see through the slit in the bedroom curtain. It was still dark outside. He glanced at the clock next to the bed. It was 5:00 a.m. He should have been up an hour ago. He grimaced and reached for the cellular phone on the nightstand. He needed to reach Dr. Baker. With a finger, Ross managed to dial 1 on his speed dial. The answering service picked up on the third ring.

"Dr. Baker, please," Ross said. He grimaced again.

"I'm sorry, Mr. Kincaid," Maggie said. "Dr. Baker is out of town for the next couple of days. He's attending a funeral up in Houston. Dr. Phillips is covering for him."

"When did he leave?" Ross inquired.

"Last night," Maggie answered.

"I see."

"Would you like for me to leave a message for Dr. Phillips?"

Ross couldn't believe his luck. The woman he didn't want to see the most was On Call.

"Mr. Kincaid, are you still there?" Maggie prompted. "Would you like for me to get in contact with Dr. Phillips?"

Ross didn't have a choice. Remain in pain or face Nikki. "Okay, put a call in to Dr. Phillips. It's a medical emergency."

"Can you please be more specific?"

"No. Just tell Dr. Phillips to get here quickly," Ross said.

"Yes, Mr. Kincaid. I will relay the message to Dr. Phillips."

* * *

Thirty minutes later, Nikki arrived at the manor. She didn't get much information from Maggie, except that Ross Kincaid had called, said it was an emergency, and asked for her to come as quick as possible.

Nikki exited the taxi and hurried up to the door. As she was about to knock, she ran into Blake on his way out.

"Whoa. Good morning, Doc," Blake exclaimed. "What brings you here so early in the morning?"

"I'm here to see Ross," Nikki explained.

Blake smiled a mischievous smile. "Really."

Nikki picked up on his meaning. "No. He called Dr. Baker's answering service this morning and said it was a medical emergency."

Blake's smile slipped. He looked toward his brother's room. "Oh no. He got tossed pretty hard yesterday." He rushed to the stairs, taking two at a time.

Nikki followed.

Blake made it to Ross's bedroom in no time. He knocked on the door. Franklin Sr. and Junior spilled out into the hallway.

"What is it?" a panicked Franklin Sr. asked.

"It's Ross," Blake explained. "He called Dr. Baker's answering service this morning. Some kind of emergency." When Ross didn't answer, he used his shoulder to force the door open.

They entered the room to find Ross lying face up on top of the covers. He was topless, only wearing blue pajama bottoms.

Blake and his father rushed to his side. Junior remained in the doorway, a blank expression on his face.

"Ross? Ross? What is it, son?" Franklin Sr. asked in a worried tone. "Is it your neck? Back?"

Nikki tapped Franklin Sr. on the arm to allow her to get closer to examine Ross. "Step aside, Mr. Kincaid."

She leaned down next to the bed. Ross was alert. His eyes followed her movements. He seemed to hear everything going on around him.

"Ross, can you hear me?" Ross nodded.

"Where are you in pain?"

"My back," Ross answered. "Feels like it's on fire. I can't move."

"Have you had problems with your back?"

"Yes." Ross answered. "But it's not related to the fall. It's a sciatic nerve."

"Thanks for the information but let me take a look."

"No!" Ross exclaimed. "No examination!"

Nikki leaned back in surprise.

"Ross, how can I properly diagnose you if I don't examine you?"

"Dr. Baker gives me a muscle relaxer and something for the pain. I'm back in the saddle in no time."

"I'm not Dr. Baker," Nikki answered. "I don't give medications without examining the patient. Tell me what happened."

"I can appreciate that, Doc," Ross said with emphasis.

"I can tell you," Blake said. "He's getting ready for the Invitational. He has been riding the mechanical bull like a mad man. He got tossed. Hard. More than once."

"Be quiet, Blake," Ross snapped.

"Hardhead," Blake mumbled. "See if I run up those stairs again to check on ya," he whined. "Don't even appreciate it." He headed for the door.

"You're paying for a new door," Ross said after him.

"No, I'm not," Blake yelled back.

Ross refocused on Nikki. "Well, Doc, do I get a shot, or do I just lie here in pain?"

"Ross, mind your manners," Franklin Sr. exclaimed. "The doctor here is just doing her job. So why don't you let her take a look at ya?"

"Because I already know what is wrong with me," Ross said.

"When did you get a medical license?" Nikki threw back at him. "I'm the one with an M.D. behind her name, not you." She motioned for Franklin Sr. to step out into the hallway with her.

"What is it, Doc?" Franklin Sr. asked.

"What can you tell me? Because as you can see, he's not going to give me anything."

"He's telling the truth. Dr. Baker does give him a muscle relaxer for the flare-ups. But if I were you, I would call up Doc Baker to get the whole story. My son is not being honest about everything."

"I was going to call him anyway. Now is as good a time as any. Thanks, Mr. Kincaid."

"No problem," Franklin Sr. said before heading back into Ross's room.

Nikki took out her cellular phone and placed a call to Dr. Baker. He confirmed the sciatic nerve flare-ups and the steroid epidural shot that he prescribed for the pain. He filled her in on the neck injury and the fact that one wrong fall and Ross could be paralyzed. Nikki rushed to the clinic. Dr. Baker had given her the information that she needed, but she wanted to see Ross's records for herself. Men in Ross's field were prone to life- threatening injuries. The adrenaline and love for what they did outweighed the danger. She had treated many patients like him. No amount of talking would sway them. You just had to pray that they have a safe ride. She looked at Ross's chart. Dr. Baker had kept detailed records. After reviewing them herself, she agreed with his findings. He had a history of falls, breaks, bumps, and bruises over the years. She wondered how he could still get on a horse.

Twenty minutes later, she knocked, and entered Ross's room. Lena was at his bedside. She was holding Ross's hand and whispering to him in a comforting tone. She wanted to tell her to leave and not in a nice way. Ross seemed to be enjoying her presence.

"Did you bring the muscle relaxer?" Lena snapped.

"Yes, I did."

"Hurry and give it to him," Lena yelled. "Can't you see he's in pain?"

"Lena." Ross grimaced. "I told you I'm fine. Nikki had to confirm with Dr. Baker." He glanced at Nikki. "Am I right?"

"You are right, Ross."

"It's Mr. Kincaid," Lena added.

"I asked Nikki to call me Ross," he said.

Nikki ignored the outburst. "And I took a few minutes to look at your records to familiarize myself with your case." She could feel Lena watching her every move. She thought about what Junior said, that he and Lena had watched them together.

"Very thorough." Ross said.

"Like I said, I don't like to give medications unless I know what's going on with the patient."

"Do you know what you're doing?" Lena asked with sarcasm.

Nikki ignored her again. She didn't like to use her authority as a physician, but the woman was getting on her last nerve. "Lena, do you mind stepping outside a moment so that I can take care of the patient?"

Lena blinked. "Yes, I do mind."

"Lena?" Ross replied. "It's only for a minute."

Lena glared at Nikki. She began to say something, then thought better of it.

"You can wait outside in the hall," Nikki said with satisfaction. "It won't take long."

"Then why can't I stay?" Lena whined.

"Because I need to examine him," Nikki explained. She thought she would get an argument from Ross, but to her surprise he remained silent.

Lena raised her nose in the air and reluctantly strolled out. "She doesn't mean anything by it," Ross said.

"Yes, she does," Nikki quipped. Lena was used to getting what she wanted no matter whom it hurt. "Where can I wash up?"

Ross nodded toward the private bath. She stepped inside a room twice the size of her bathroom. It was decorated in all blue. Her favorite color. She quickly washed her hands, squeezed sanitizer on them, and returned to her patient.

Nikki slipped her hands into a pair of gloves. She opened the black medical bag and removed a syringe filled with medication. "I'm going to give you an epidural spinal injection of cortisone. Where do you want it?" she teased.

Ross looked alarmed. "What do you mean? Dr. Baker only gives..." He stopped talking when he saw the look of amusement on her face. "Funny."

"Okay, tough guy. Are you able to turn over? Or shall I call one of your brothers?"

"I can do it." Ross grimaced but managed to flip over onto his stomach. "You are enjoying this, aren't you?" he asked.

"I don't enjoy seeing anyone in pain," Nikki answered. "I'm sure Dr. Baker spoke to you about surgery for your damaged disc."

"Yes. He did."

"Then he explained to you the alternatives, like minimally invasive decompression surgery. The surgeon removes the damaged disc that is pressing up against the nerve to release pressure and reduce the symptoms."

"I'm thinking about it," Ross said.

"What is there to think about? It's a small incision, and none of your muscles will be affected," Nikki explained. "You should consider it instead of the shots."

"Not while I'm still competing," Ross answered.

"I hope you change your mind," she said as she prepared to sanitize the area and inject the medicine into his lower back. She had to admit it was hard to concentrate with a half-naked Ross. The hard muscles in his back were pleasant to look at. She envisioned herself, rubbing her hands up and down his back.

"Like what you see?" Ross asked, looking up at her face.

Nikki could see the smoldering heat in his eyes.

"Not bad to look at, I admit," Nikki answered. "But you see one naked body, you've seen them all."

"Not in my case, sweetheart," Ross said. "I'm one of a kind." His eyes locked with hers.

"Blake!" she yelled, never taking her eyes off Ross. "Are you still out there?"

"Still here," Blake answered, rushing into the room.

"You can be my assistant. Can you stand by in case I need you?" Nikki said not trusting herself being alone with him.

"Sure,"

"We will pick this up later," Ross said with a smile.

Chapter Nine

The next morning, Nikki rolled out of bed. She quickly dressed and made her way downstairs for her morning coffee. Her body was craving it to start the day. Before she went to work, she planned to check on Ross. Nikki slid into her favorite booth next to the window and yawned.

"Good morning, Doc," Mabelle said, placing the cup in front of her. "Here's your usual."

"Thanks. I need it."

"How's Ross?"

"How did you—" Nikki began. "I forgot, this is a small town. I see the gossip pipeline is in full effect. Ross is just fine."

"Will he be able to compete in the Invitational?"

"He should be if he follows doctor's orders."

"Well, make sure that he does. We are rooting for him to win again this year."

"I'll do my best."

"Do you want anything besides coffee?"

"No. Just coffee."

"It's a good thing that you were there. With you he is in good hands. Do you know who will be taking Doc's place?"

"The clinic has other physicians on staff who are more than qualified to take his place."

"How much longer do you have to work at the clinic?"

"Only a couple more days."

The bell above the door jingled and Lilly strolled in. Nikki noticed her hair color had gone from blue to red. But it was styled in a nice, short bob that fit her face perfectly. They looked at each other and smiled.

"Lilly, I love your hair color." Nikki said. "It says attitude."

"I wanted to try something new."

"Headed to work, Lilly?" Mabelle asked.

"Yeah, I'm running late. Misty is going to kill me. I figured if I can pick up a couple of those blueberry muffins that she likes, then she might not notice."

"Wait a moment," Mabelle said. "I'll bag a few for you."

Lilly slid in the booth across from Nikki. She leaned across the table. "How's Ross?"

"Ross is fine. Have you spoken to Blake since that night?"

"Not one word from that little twerp. When you see him, tell him to lose my number."

"I will." Nikki giggled.

"Good news. I might be heading to New York," Lilly said. "A friend of my mother's has a chain of beauty shops. She asked me to send her my resume. Wish me luck."

"You won't need it," Nikki said. "The job is as good as yours."

"I hope so," Lilly said as Mabelle returned with a bag of muffins. She stood. "I'd better get going. I will keep you posted."

Nikki gave her thumbs up.

Lilly rushed out the door and down the sidewalk. "You will be here for the Invitational?" Mabelle asked.

"Yes. I'm leaving the next day," Nikki said. "My car is fixed. I just need to pick it up."

"What about Ross?" Mabelle asked.

Nikki frowned. "What about him?"

"Aren't you two an item?" Mabelle asked.

"No, we're not. Is that on the gossip pipeline?"

"You could say that," Mabelle replied.

"This time the pipeline is wrong."

"The pipeline is never wrong, honey."

"It is this time," Nikki argued.

"If you say so," Mabelle said. "Oh, we talked Zack into going to see a doctor," She changed the subject. "Jubal took him himself."

"And?"

"You were right." Mabelle's tone lowered. "The cough wasn't good. Lung Cancer."

"Is it terminal?" Nikki asked. Mabelle nodded. "Terminal."

* * *

An hour later, Nikki walked outside in the cool, crisp morning air. She stood in front of the boarding house. Suddenly, a green Jeep Cherokee pulled up in front of her. The windows rolled down, revealing that it was Lena behind the wheel.

She rolled her eyes. "I don't have time for this, Lena. It's too early in the morning."

"I want to offer you a ride," Lena said. "We need to talk."

"No, we don't. I'll wait for a taxi. One should be here any moment."

"It will be much faster if you let me give you a ride. I'm going out to the manor anyway," Lena relayed. "Ross is having his follow-up appointment this morning. You don't want to keep his waiting, do you?"

Every time she saw Lena, she was more convinced why she didn't like her. There was no way she was Ross's type. She was positive the more he resisted her advances, the more Lena was attracted to him. And Lena was the type of woman who didn't allow anything or anyone getting in her way.

"Don't tell me that you're afraid of little ole me?"

"Little girl, trust me, I am not afraid of you."

Lena put on a pair of expensive shades. "Get in, old lady."

Nikki reluctantly opened the door and slid into the passenger's seat. The two women rode in silence a few minutes. The sound of country music filled the interior of the truck. Nikki looked out the window; scenes of farms and windmills zoomed by. She glanced over at Lena, who seemed to be focused on the road. Nikki was uncomfortable with the silence. She was the first to speak. "What do you want to talk to me about?"

Lena stole a look at Nikki. "I think you know."

"If I knew I wouldn't ask."

"It's about the other day."

"What about it? Wait. Is it about me asking you to leave the room? Because if it is, I was just doing my job as his doctor. I had every right to do so," Nikki said. "You're not a relative."

"Not yet."

"Well, when and if you do become a family member, you will be able to stay."

"Thanks."

Nikki knew the answer to her next question. She just wanted to hear it from Lena. "You like Ross?"

"Since I was ten years old," Lena answered. "We'd just moved here. Some of our cattle got mixed up with the Kincaid's. My eyes landed on this tall, dark, and handsome cowboy who came to round them up. It was love at first sight for me."

"You don't believe that, do you?"

"Yes, I do. I mean, he looks serious all the time and can be stubborn as all get-out. But Ross Kincaid is the man for me."

"Does he know that?"

"Of course."

"Then why aren't you two together?"

"Who says we're not?"

"The town gossip pipeline says he's single and has been since he broke up with his fiancée," Nikki replied.

"Those busybodies don't know everything."

"I don't know; they have been right on the money since I've been here. If Ross was off the market, I'm sure that would be the town news."

"They are right about one thing." Lena looked sad. "Ross was devastated when Hailey married someone else. She smashed his little ole heart into a million pieces. He was out of it for quite a while. He began competing in every rodeo that he could and won. He was gone for months at a time."

"That explains how he became the best in the country," Nikki said. "Was Ross not riding before?"

"He'd compete in an event here and there, mostly local shows," Lena explained. "But after Hailey left that all changed. It was like he put all his pain into riding. It was his way of dealing with everything."

"I know a lot of people who use pain as a motivator," Nikki said. "Sounds like that's what Ross did. How he dealt with everything."

"I believe so."

"It worked. He's the National Champion."

"At what price?"

"You're talking about his spinal cord injury?"

Lena nodded. "You saw him the other day. He couldn't even move. When he was injured several years back, he was out of commission for over a year. It almost killed him, not to be able to ride."

"Why are you telling me all of this?" Nikki asked. "I saw his records. His injury is not as bad as people think it is. Besides, except for a few bruises, he has been very careful."

"Careful?" Lena exclaimed. "He was wearing protective gear and still suffered a nasty fall. With his neck snapping like that, who knows what effect it's having on him. All he needs is another nasty fall and he's in a wheelchair."

"Dr. Baker keeps clearing him."

"All he does is keep telling Ross to be careful."

"As doctors, that's all we can do under the circumstances. If he is medically able to compete, we can't stop him."

"I was afraid of that," Lena said. "Don't think because I told you all of that I like you."

"Then why are you telling me?"

"You're his doctor. Just because he is nice to you doesn't mean that he likes you. So, stop batting those beautiful brown eyes at him. Ross Kincaid is mine."

"Lena, there is nothing going on between Ross and me," Nikki explained. "To be honest, I'm sick and tired of people saying that there is. He is just a patient. Besides, I'm leaving in a couple of days. I can assure you that you have nothing to worry about."

"Keep it that way. Do your time at the clinic and go."

"Is that an order?"

"Yes, it is," Lena said as she pulled in front of the manor.

Nikki faced Lena. "I don't like being threatened."

"I don't care. Now get out."

Without another word, Nikki climbed out of the truck. Flabbergasted, she watched as Lena burned rubber away from the manor.

She looked up at Ross's window. The curtain was drawn. Her heart kicked into high gear as she thought about how he looked at her the other day. Being in his presence had kept her up late into the night. She finally dropped off around 3:00 a.m.

Nikki headed inside and hurried up the stairway to Ross's room. As she walked down the hallway, she heard spurs. She looked to see Junior coming from the last room on the right. She stopped in front of him. "Good morning, Junior," she said.

"Morning." Junior returned her greeting. He continued walking.

Nikki's heart dropped. She turned around. "Junior?"

Junior stopped in his tracks.

Nikki walked up behind him. "Why are you acting like this?"

"Acting like what?"

"Us not speaking. Talking to each other. You haven't called me back."

"I spoke. Far as us talking, I have nothing to say," Junior replied. "I'm no one's sloppy second." He continued down the hall and stairs.

"I told you that it's not like that," Nikki said, trailing him.

"I don't believe you." Junior swung around to face her. "The only one that is not admitting the truth here," he pointed to Nikki, "is you." He continued down the stairs.

Nikki looked to see Franklin Sr. standing at the bottom of the steps.

Nikki nodded. She headed back toward Ross's room. As she was about to knock on the door, Blake appeared in the hallway.

"Are you here to check on Ross?"

"Yes."

"He will like that," Blake said. "I know I would. Head on in." Nikki knocked twice and waited for a response. It was quiet.

"Are you sure he's inside?"

"He should be," Blake replied. He knocked, then threw open the door. "Ross. Dr. Phillips... He's not here."

Nikki rushed inside. "What? Where could he have gone so early in the morning? He's supposed to be on bed rest for the next couple of days."

"Bed rest? Ross? Not likely," Blake said.

Nikki hurried from the room. She zoomed down the stairs and ran into Franklin Sr. once again. "Have you seen Ross?"

Franklin Sr. leaned back. "Good morning to you, too, Dr. Phillips."

Nikki was sorry that he saw the argument between her and Junior. "Good morning, Mr. Kincaid. I'm sorry. I'm just concerned about my patient. Have you seen Ross?"

"He's out in the barn," Franklin Sr. answered.

"The barn?" Nikki exclaimed. "He is on bed rest." She stomped toward the barn. She hurried inside to find Ross throwing bales of hay. She could not believe it. Lena said he was stubborn as all get out, and she was right. She placed her hands on her hips. "Ross Kincaid!"

Ross was startled. He stopped in mid-stride and turned around. The look of surprise on his face almost made her laugh.

"You are supposed to be on bed rest for the next couple of days. What are you doing?"

Ross continued carrying bales of hay. "I can't lie around. This is a ranch. There is a lot to do."

"Not for you. You have two other brothers," Nikki explained. "You need to rest or you will aggravate your back again."

Ross turned and looked at Nikki. His eyes traveled in a subtle way from the top of her head to her breasts and down to her feet. She wanted to cross her arms over her chest to head off the course of heat pushing through her body at his open look. Her eyes locked with his. Her mouth went dry when she realized he was not wearing a shirt. The blue denim jeans encased his hips and powerful strong legs. She thought she would die when he pushed his hat back. He removed the black bandana from around his neck and dabbed at the sweat on his forehead. It was a simple but sensual gesture.

"I promise not to overdo it."

Nikki managed to regain her composure. "If I had a dime for every time a patient told me that, I would be rich."

"The Invitational is soon. I'm wound up; I have to keep my mind and body busy."

"Look, Ross, I understand, but if you want me to clear you, you have to be on bed rest."

Ross tried to speak.

"That means no work around the ranch for the next couple of days," Nikki finished.

"For the next couple of days, huh?" Ross removed the tan work gloves.

This time, it was Nikki whose eyes took a trip over his well-proportioned, glistening body. She felt a pool of liquid between her legs. She struggled to look away. "That's right. Couple of days," she stammered out. "I mean the Invitational is this weekend. You still have a couple of days to get some practice in. I know it may be difficult for a man like you to do, but it's called 'rest'—do it." She turned to leave.

"How about dinner?" Ross asked out of the blue.

Nikki stopped in her tracks. She twirled around. Did Ross Kincaid just ask her out on a date? Did she hear him wrong? It was one thing to flirt with him but to go out with him was another. Especially since she has been seen around town with Junior. But she had to keep things real. She couldn't deny her feelings for him. She wanted to go out with him. Be with him.

"Can you give me an answer?" Ross prompted.

Nikki answered his question with one of her own. "Is there a nice restaurant in this town?"

Ross chuckled. "What kind of food do you like?" "French."

"We don't have French restaurants around here, but we've got loads of great barbecue places."

"Hmmm, barbecue, is it as good as what your chef prepared?" "No, but Clint's barbecue comes in a close second," Ross replied. "I have to warn you, it's spicy." "The spicier, the better."

"I'll keep that in mind," Ross said. "So how about it? Spicy barbecue at Clint's. Say eight o'clock tonight. I'll pick you up at Mabelle's."

"I'll be ready."

Ross's face broke into a big, sloppy grin. "Great, I'll see you then." He walked her outside the barn. "You'd better get going to the clinic. Dr. Baker is returning today."

"What? He's not due back until the weekend."

"All I know is that he phoned Father last night and said he was returning today. It could be because you are leaving in the next couple of days. He wanted to be here."

Nikki's heart dropped in her stomach. "That could be."

Ross shifted from one feet to the other. "I mean, your car is ready. You have faithfully done your time."

"Yes," Nikki said. "Two days and counting. I'm done paying off my debts to the Kincaids."

"You don't have to sound so happy about it."

"I'm not," Nikki said in a coy tone.

"Will you at least stick around for the Invitational?"

Nikki smiled. "I would love to see the great Ross Kincaid in action. Also, my best friend is on her way. I want to be here."

"I remember you mentioning her," Ross said. "Her and her family are on the way here."

An awkward silence fell. She could feel the strong chemistry between them. Ross's eyes found hers. She couldn't look away. No words were needed. He stepped toward her.

He hesitated a moment, as if he were seeking permission. She leaned in, letting him know it was okay. Nikki closed her eyes. A moment later, she could taste the sweetness of his lips on hers.

The kiss was gentle, then increased in intensity. Wave after wave from it set her body aflame. She could feel it from the top of her head down to the bottom of her feet. She always thought that Winston was a good kisser, but Ross's know-how was on a different level. His tongue expertly mingled with hers. She angled her head and thrust her tongue deeper. She couldn't help herself. The kiss mixed with the sounds of Ross's moaning was intoxicating.

Ross was the first to pull away. "Whew," he exclaimed. He touched his lips with a hand. "I figured you to be a good kisser. But..."

Her head fell into his broad naked chest. She snuggled up to him. "Really."

"I'm glad, that I wasn't wrong."

"Same here, cowboy," Nikki replied. She took his hand in hers. "What are we doing here, Ross?"

"I don't know, Nikki, but I like it."

She loved the way he enunciated her name. "Me too. I like it when you call me Nikki."

Ross reached up and removed a strand of hair from her face.

He tucked it behind her ear. "Not as much as I like saying it."

Nikki was the first to compose herself. "I better get going before I kidnap you for the day."

"That may not be a bad idea," Ross agreed.

Nikki looked up in his face. "We'll talk about it later, after dinner." She turned and headed toward the clinic. As she walked away, she could feel Ross's eyes on her back side. She looked back to make sure that he was watching. He was grinning from ear-to-ear. For good measure, she added a little more twist to her walk.

* * *

Ross felt like he was walking on a cloud. He threw his hat up in the air. He felt like a schoolboy with a crush. He glanced over at the hired hands who gave him thumbs up. He turned and strolled back in the barn.

"So, you are seeing Nikki behind my back?"

Ross turned to see Junior coming through the door. He briskly walked up to him. He could see Junior was doing his best to control his anger.

"You knew I had interest in her, and you still went for her," Junior exclaimed.

"Yes, I did," Ross said. "I got word from her that the two of you were only friends. That makes her fair game."

Junior blinked. "We could be much more if you bow out."

Ross smirked. "I'm not going to do that. She wants my attention. You'd better stay away from her."

"Or what?" Junior inquired. He covered the small space between them. "What are you going to do? You going to beat me up?"

The scene was like two gladiators in an arena getting ready to do battle.

"I will fight for what is mine, brother or not," Ross threw back.

"What's going on?" Franklin Sr. asked, walking inside.

Blake brought up the rear. "I can hear you yelling all the way up the hill."

Ross never took his eyes off Junior. "Nothing, it's just a little misunderstanding."

"Little?" Junior exclaimed. "You call kissing my girl little?"

"Kiss?" Franklin Sr. inquired. "Who did he kiss?"

"She is not your girl, Junior. Get it straight," Ross replied.

"If I see you anywhere near her again, so help me..." Junior began. "I'll—"

"You'll what?" Ross countered.

"You're trying to take her away from me, just like you did with Hailey."

Ross straightened. "What does Hailey have to do with this?"

"Everything, you bastard," Junior said. He followed it with a punch to Ross's abdomen.

Ross doubled over from the blow. The Kincaid men have had their shares of fights but never over a woman. "What was that for?" He groaned before coming up with a right uppercut to Juniors' jaw.

Junior retaliated by hitting Ross so hard in the face, he tripped backward over a bale of hay.

Ross quickly stumbled to his feet and lunged at Junior.

Both men landed with a loud thud. Ross quickly maneuvered himself atop Junior and began punching him in the face.

Junior covered himself from the blows.

Ross found himself being pulled off by Blake and Franklin Sr.

"Boys. Boys. Cut this out, right now," Franklin Sr. ordered. "You're brothers. Family. I raised you better than that."

Ross and Junior came to their feet. They glared at each other.

"Your mother is probably turning over in her grave," Franklin Sr. continued.

"Tell that to him," Junior massaged his right jaw. "He has come between a woman and me, not once but twice."

"What the hell are you talking about? What does this have to do with Hailey?"

Junior checked his jaw. Without another word, he turned on his heels and rushed out the barn.

"Junior!" Ross yelled after him.

"What was all that about?" Franklin Sr. asked.

Ross forcibly removed his work gloves. "I don't know, but I am sure as hell going to find out." He rushed out after his brother.

"Ross!" Franklin Sr. said to his retreating figure.

* * *

"I can't wait to see you, Corina," Nikki said into the phone. "I know we talk almost every day, but I'm looking forward to seeing your smiling face."

"Me, too," Corina answered. "The plane lands at 10 in the morning. The ranch is sending a shuttle to pick us up. I am excited!" She squealed. "David is coming, too."

"I know," Nikki said. "I can't wait to see him. We have so much to discuss. The three of us here together reminds me of old times." Silence fell between them. "Have you seen Winston?" she finally asked.

"I saw him last week. That slimy snake came slithering into my office. He asked about you."

Nikki heart skipped a beat. "Really?" No matter how much she tried to deny it, she still had feelings for Winston. The man was still in her system. She knew that in due time that she would get over him. Going out with Ross was a step in the right direction.

"What did he say?"

"He wanted to know where you were," Corina answered. "What did you tell him?"

"What do you think I said to him?" Corina replied. "I told him the truth, that you were dating a hot, hunky cowboy. You should have seen the look on his face. It was magic." She hissed. "Please don't tell me you still have feelings for him."

"No. No. Nothing like that. Call it curiosity."

"Curiosity my eye. You have moved on."

"I know," Nikki said.

Corina gasped. "How is Ross? Tell me everything, and don't leave anything out."

Nikki could feel the heat wash over her cheeks. The sweet nectar of Ross's lips on hers was still fresh in her mind.

"We sort of kissed."

"Sort of kissed?" Corina asked. "How do you sort of kiss? You either kiss or you don't."

"Did we ever." Nikki was still reeling from the effects.

"I said tell me everything…" Corina began. "Who is the better kisser? Winston or Ross?"

"Corina, I cannot believe you, that is such a juvenile question," Nikki said out of embarrassment.

"Which one?" Corina prompted.

"I have to give it to Ross," Nikki replied. "He is a great kisser. I swear the earth under my feet moved. No man has ever kissed me like that. Honestly, I could kiss those beautiful lips all day, every day."

"I'm sure you want to do more than kiss him."

"You're so bad."

"Don't tell me you haven't thought about it."

"I couldn't help it," Nikki confessed.

"What about Junior? I thought you guys were getting along." Nikki looked to see her next patient being placed in the examination room. "I'll fill you in when you get here. My next patient is here. Smooches," she said, and ended the call.

* * *

Ross found Junior down by Sumner Creek. He was skipping stones. He knew he would find him here. Since he was a little boy, he would always come here when he was feeling down. He carefully watched his brother before approaching. The last time they had a disagreement was in grade school when they fought over a bag of Skittles. That was nothing like what had just happened over Nikki. While she was worth it, he didn't want it to come between him and his brother. He was also curious to find out about Hailey. He stepped on a twig. Juniors' head snapped around. He gave a deep sigh but didn't acknowledge Ross. He continued skipping stones.

Ross carefully stood next to him. He bent down and picked up a rock. He joined Junior in skipping. The awkwardness between them was intense. It lasted for at least five minutes. Junior was the first to speak. "Why didn't you tell me that you were interested?"

Ross threw another rock. "I didn't know I was; it just snuck up on me."

"Doesn't make it right," Junior said.

"Never said it did."

"You knew how I felt about her. You should have been man enough to tell me the truth or just walked away. You're so damn good at everything."

"That's not true."

"Yes, it is," Junior argued. "In school, you got the better grades. I struggled. You were captain of the football team. I rode the bench. You went off to college and graduated top of your class. I stayed home. Now you are the best rodeo rider in the nation, and once again you get the girl. I can't compete."

Ross glanced at Junior in disbelief. "I'm sorry, Junior. I never knew you felt this way."

"Of course, you didn't."

"We can't let women come between us. We are family. Blood."

"It's too late for that," Junior replied. "Women have already has come between us."

Ross drew his eyebrows together. "What did you mean about Hailey?"

Junior removed his hat. "Does it matter?"

"Of course, it matters. If I would have known, I—"

Junior cut him off. "Would have done the same. It's who you are."

"That is not true. This is the first time I am hearing that you had feelings for Hailey. We should talk about this. Get everything out in the open."

Junior threw another stone in the pond. "I don't want to talk about it, not now." He turned to walk away.

Ross halted his movement.

"Take your hand off me," Junior replied.

Ross slowly removed his hand. "Junior?"

"I have things to do," he said and hurried off toward the manor.

Ross stood there for a moment, trying to take in what had happened. Regardless of how he felt about Nikki, he didn't want her to come between him and his brother.

* * *

Nikki moved around the room at top speed. She was excited about her date with Ross. She got off work at the clinic early. On the way home, she stopped into Her Style Boutique and purchased a beautiful, sleeveless lavender dress for the occasion. She placed her hands on her hips and walked over to the dresser mirror. She decided this time to wear her hair down. She glanced at her watch. It was five minutes until eight o'clock. Ross was due in five minutes.

Thirty minutes past and Ross had not shown up. One hour later and still no Ross. *If he could not make it, he could at least give me a call,* she thought. She did not want to be forward, but she wanted to know why Ross had not phoned. She grabbed her phone and punched in his number. The call went to voicemail. She sent a text.

Fifteen more minutes passes and still no response from Ross. At ten o'clock she undressed and tossed the dress in the box, along with the shoes. She was disappointed. There had to be a good reason why he had not kept their date or responded. She plopped down on the foot of the bed and folded her legs underneath her. She hoped he was all right. Nikki could not believe her luck with men. What was wrong with her? Within the last couple of weeks, she had been dumped by two men.

She fell back on the bed. She drew her legs up into a fetal position. She couldn't help but imagine herself as an old maid in a house full of cats.

* * *

Ross stretched out on the king-size bed, his hands behind his neck and long legs crossed at the ankles. He re-read the text messages from Nikki. He wanted to tell her what was going on, but he didn't have the guts. He listened to the voicemail again. "Ross, call me. Tell me what is going on. I hope you are okay." He placed the phone on the nightstand. He felt bad. Nikki sounded hurt. He never meant to hurt her. He was having a bad day—Junior telling him they shared two women and him standing up a date.

He stood. It was him who initiated the first move. She didn't do anything to deserve the treatment she was getting from him. The least he could do was apologize. Ross strolled over to the large walk-in closet. He removed a pair of black running shoes and stepped into them. He removed a blue windbreaker, slipped his arms into it, and put a baseball cap on his head.

Ross hurried down the stairs. He ran into Blake on the way up.

"Where are you headed in such a hurry?"

"I have something to take care of," he threw over his right shoulder on his way out the door.

"Ross, we need to talk," Franklin Sr. said, exiting the Mercedes.

Ross headed toward his truck. "Can't it wait?" he replied. "I have someplace I have to be."

"You're going to see that doctor, aren't you?"

"What if I am?"

"She has been nothing but trouble since she got here," Franklin Sr. explained. "Tearing down the fence, showing affection to you and your brother. Her and Junior fighting. You and your brother fighting." He huffed. "I won't have it. I just returned from seeing Judge Spears. I am dropping the charges. I want Dr. Phillips out of here. The sooner the better. I've already told Dr. Baker that she can go."

"You had no right to do that," Ross replied.

"The hell I didn't. I had every right," Franklin Sr. said. "It is my fence. My clinic. It is me she owes the money to. I refuse to have my boys fighting like a bunch of 10-year-old on the playground over some woman. Besides, she is leaving in a couple of days anyway."

Ross heard enough. He opened the door of the truck and slid behind the steering wheel. He had to talk to Nikki before Dr. Baker. He couldn't let her leave without telling her the truth about what had happened between them.

Franklin Sr. strolled over to the vehicle. He knocked on the passenger-side window with the end of a cane. "Ross, come to your senses. Let her go."

Ross ignored him. He put the truck in drive and sped off.

* * *

"I'm sorry to drop by so late," Dr. Baker said, moving further in the room. "But I wanted you to hear the good news from me."

"Good news?"

"Yes. Franklin Sr. spoke to Judge Spears. He dropped the charges against you. You are free to go."

Nikki leaned back. "Just like that?" she asked. "I can go?" "Franklin Sr. called me himself. I checked it out with Judge

Spear, and he confirmed it. You can be on your way any time you like."

Nikki dropped her eyes. She clasped her hands together.

"I thought you would be more excited. You have been saying you were ready to go since you arrived. Has something happened to change your mind?"

"No. Don't be silly," Nikki answered in a flat tone. "It's just that the news comes as a surprise."

"Is there anything you want to talk about?"

"Like what?"

"I don't know. You tell me."

Nikki managed a straight face. "I have nothing to say except that I am ready to get out of this town." She strolled over to the clothes rack. "My car is repaired. I was just working off my debt," she mumbled under her breath. "Now that it is cancelled there is nothing keeping me here." She pulled out her suitcase and began throwing clothes into it.

"No one said you had to leave tonight," Dr. Baker said.

"I'm just getting prepared."

"What are you going to do in Montgomery? Any ideas?"

"Not right now."

"Well, if you need anything... A reference? A friend? A shoulder to cry on? Give me a call." Dr. Baker headed toward the door.

"Thanks, Dr. Baker, for everything."

"It was my pleasure, Dr. Phillips. I hope everything works out well for you." He opened the door and came face to face with Ross.

"Dr. Baker, what are you doing here?"

"I imagine the same thing as you."

Ross looked away. "Yes. I need to talk to Nikki. Dr. Phillips," he quickly corrected himself.

"Well, Nikki doesn't want to talk to you," Nikki said, behind Dr. Baker.

"Nikki, let me explain." Ross strolled further in the room.

"I don't remember inviting you in," Nikki barked. "So, get out!"

Ross leaned back. "You're not going to let me explain?"

"I don't want to hear it."

"I didn't mean to stand you up," Ross said. "I wanted to keep our date but Junior and I got into it."

"You and Junior? Why?"

Ross cleared his throat. "He saw us kissing. We had words and the next thing I know we were going at it."

Nikki let out a deep sigh. "You decided not to keep our date."

Ross shuffled from one foot to the other. "I didn't think it would be right to see you after that."

Nikki felt like her heart broke into a million pieces. "Now I know why Franklin Sr. spoke to the judge. His sons fighting over a woman. Not proper," she said with sarcasm. She glanced at Ross. He appeared uncomfortable. "You don't want to take things further?"

"I think things should calm down for now. Don't you?"

"Thanks for coming over to tell me in person." She walked over to the other side of the room and pretended to place the lid back on the box. Her hands were shaking. She nervously turned to face Ross. He looked away, twirling the hat in his hands. She looked past him to see Dr. Baker standing quietly in the back of the room. She had been so busy arguing with Ross she hadn't realized that he was still there. Dr. Baker's eyes met hers. Without another word, he strolled out the door.

"I didn't think it would turn out like this," Ross continued. "I'm sorry."

"What did you think would happen?" Nikki asked. "I'm leaving anyways."

"What about your friends?"

"They're coming in tomorrow morning," Nikki explained. "I'll see them before I leave. Not that it is any of your business. "Anything else, Ross?" She marched over to the door and opened it.

"No. Nothing." He headed to the door with slumped shoulders. "Good night, Nikki."

Nikki slammed the door behind him. She threw herself on the bed. She was hurt. She was upset but she refused to cry. Not this time…

Chapter Ten

The next morning, Nikki threw on a pair of black jeans, a white tee shirt, and cowboy boots. She rushed into the bathroom. She splashed cold water on her face, brushed her teeth, and pulled her hair back into a ponytail. She got up the nerve to look in the mirror and jumped back in horror. She was done crying over men. Winston and Ross could suck eggs for all she cared. She grabbed the cowboy hat off the dresser, placed it on her head, and dashed out the door.

Once she arrived home in Montgomery, she was sure that she would be able to find a job. She might even open her own practice. The sky was the limit. Getting fired was the best thing to happen in her life. "Yes," she exclaimed, pumping a fist in the air for encouragement. She arrived in front of the lodge just as the shuttle pulled up. She wrung her hands in anticipation. Guests began to dismount, and then Corina, her husband, and their two sons came into view.

Nikki squealed when she saw her, throwing her arms around her neck. The two women rocked in excitement.

"Corina, it's so good to see you."

"Me, too. I couldn't sleep at all last night."

Corina's husband, Oscar, cleared his throat. "Excuse me, ladies. The boys and I are here."

The women giggled.

"I know, Oscar. We didn't mean to ignore you. How have you been?"

"Fine. Thank you. It is good to see you, Nikki. How have you been?"

"Great." Nikki focused on Taylor and Tyler; they could almost pass for twins. "Hello, boys. Wow you guys have grown."

Tyler said hi, but Taylor was too busy looking at the horses to pay attention to her. "Horses. Mom, can we ride?"

Tyler joined in the amazement of the ranch. He tugged on Corina's shirt when the dogs, Fred and Lucy, appeared on the scene. "Look at the dogs. Can I go pet them?"

"Not right now," Corina answered. "Why don't we get checked in first and then you'll be able to ride the horses." She looked at Oscar. "See, I told you this is better than Disneyland."

Oscar looked around. "I have to admit this place is something."

He took a deep breath. "I'm loving the clean, fresh air. I am dying to see the rest of the place."

"I thought David was with you guys," Nikki said.

"I am here," the familiar voice said, coming from the shuttle. Nikki looked to see David dressed in full Western gear, including chaps. He strolled over and gave her a tight hug.

Nikki looked him up and down. "I don't believe it. What are you wearing?"

"I wanted to be prepared. Fit right in."

Nikki laughed. "Don't you think you overdid it?"

"Not at all," David said.

"I'm so happy to see all of you guys."

"We're excited to be here," David said. "You're looking good. Maybe being a cowgirl agrees with you." He glanced around the ranch. "I have to agree with Oscar. This place is something; I could get used to this."

"You look much more relaxed than the last time I saw you," Corina said. "I am loving the cowgirl outfit." She looked her up and down. "Nice."

Nikki tipped her hat at the end as she seen the brothers often do. "Thank you, ma'am," she joked. "You guys should get checked in. There is so much to see and do here." She led the group inside the lodge. She could not help but think of when Ross had given her a tour.

David checked in first, and then Corina.

"Why don't we meet back here?" David glanced at his Rolex. "Say about fifteen minutes." He reached out and grabbed her hands. "I didn't realize how much I missed you. I'm looking forward to making up for it." He pulled her into another tight embrace. "I have missed you. I wanted to say again how sorry I am."

It felt good being in David's embrace. She needed it. "Thank you, David. I needed that. Let's forget about that ugly business."

"Friends again?" David asked.

"Always," Nikki echoed.

"What is it, Nikki?" David asked. "I know that look."

"Nothing, I just..." Nikki's voice trailed off as she glanced over David's shoulder to see Ross headed in her direction. Flustered, she took a step back.

David followed her line of vision, then looked back at Nikki. He turned to look at Corina before his eyes fell on the cowboy coming toward them.

Corina strolled over and stood next to David. "Well now," she crooned.

"Indeed," David replied. "Something tells me things are about to get interesting." His eyes gave Ross the once-over. "I'm turned on and I'm a heterosexual," he said aloud

"And I am married," Corina whispered back.

Nikki gulped. Ross was dressed in full Western ensemble, including chaps, and a red bandana tied around his neck. He was looking like a tall drink of water. She wanted a sip.

With spurs jingling, Ross stopped in front of the group. "Good morning. Welcome to RFK Ranch," he said calmly in his thick Texas drawl. "You all must be Nikki's," he caught himself, "I mean, Dr. Phillip's friends."

"Yes, we must be," Corina said, "and you had it right the first time, calling her Nikki."

Ross smiled that handsome smile of his. He tipped his hat to Corina. "Thank you, ma'am."

"Ross, you didn't have to come out." Nikki said. "But since you did, let me introduce everyone. This is my best friend Corina, her husband, Oscar, and their two boys, Tyler and Taylor. This is my colleague, Dr. David Coombs. He's also a top-notch orthopedist."

Ross extended a hand to Corina's family before his eyes landed on David. "Doc, it's good to meet you. We can't have enough sawbones around here."

"Sawbones?" David repeated.

"He means another bone doctor," Nikki said, showing off. "Everyone, this is Ross Kincaid."

"I think we figured that one out," David said.

"Are you a real cowboy?" Tyler asked, looking up at Ross.

Ross pushed the hat back on his head. He knelt eye level to Tyler. "I sure am."

"Ross is being modest," Nikki added. "He's the national rodeo champ; three years running. He rides the bulls, ropes the calves, and rounds up the horses. Just like they did in the good old days."

Taylor's and Tyler's eyes lit up. "Will we get to see him ride, Mommy?"

"I hope so." Ross looked over to their parents. Corina nodded. "You rope horses, too?" Tyler asked.

Ross chuckled. He removed a glove and tousled Tyler's brown hair. "Only to break them. I rope calves for sport. You will get a chance to see while you're here. I will show you how to rope calves. Is everyone all checked in?" he asked, changing the subject.

"Yes, we are," Corina answered.

"Good. I'm happy to meet all of you. I feel like I know you all— Nikki speaks highly of y'all."

David and Corina groaned.

"Don't worry, it was all good things," Ross replied. He instructed the porters to take the luggage upstairs. "Again, it was good meeting all of you. I'm sure I will see you around." He shook their hands again before walking away.

Nikki watched as Ross vanished from view. She looked to see Corina standing with her arms folded across her chest. "Lucy, you have some 'splaining to do," she teased.

* * *

Ross hurried outside to greet the other guests. He knew there was a chance that he would run into Nikki. Seeing her again made his heart kick into full gallop. He placed a hand to his chest to check the beat. He didn't understand how one woman was able to make his blood boil. "Calm down," he said to himself. "She is leaving. Things around here will get back to normal and you won't see her again."

He looked to see the hired hand Tom headed in his direction. He had a rope draped over his right shoulder. "Everything all right, boss?"

"Yep. I'm good."

"Just checking," Tom said. He continued toward the lodge. "Uh, Tom, Dr. Phillips has some important guests that checked in today. Can you make sure they are taken care of?" Tom frowned. "We always do that, boss."

"I know. Give them a little extra on what you always give, if you understand me."

"I gotcha, boss," Tom answered. "I hear Dr. Phillips is leaving."

Ross looked off into the distance. The bright sunlight shone in his eyes. He squinted and removed a pair of shades from his shirt pocket and slipped them on. "You heard right."

"I thought she was to be here for another week."

"You thought wrong." Ross looked to see Tom eyeing him carefully.

"Sho going to miss her."

"Uh-huh," Ross said in an offhanded tone. He was determined not to show any emotions.

Tom shook his head from side to side and mumbled under his breath.

"What was that?" Ross inquired.

"Nuthin', boss."

"Have you seen Junior?" Ross asked. He hadn't come home last night or shown up for work this morning. In the past when he was to stay away from home he always called or texted his whereabouts.

"No, sir," Tom answered. "I wouldn't worry. He will show up some time. He is like a stray dog that always finds his way home. Why don't you take it easy? You have a big event coming up."

"I guess you're right," Ross replied as he headed toward the house. He strolled inside and walked across the foyer. As he was about to ascend the stairs, his cellular phone rang.

He recognized the number as belonging to Sheriff Cabot. He always phoned as a courtesy when a member of the family was in trouble.

"Hello?"

"Ross."

"What is going on, Sheriff?"

"I got Junior in my jail," Sheriff Cabot relayed. "What do you want me to do with him?"

"What is he in for?"

"Drunk, disorderly, and battery?"

"Battery?" He sighed.

"Yeah, he got all liquored up at The Big Boot last night. The person he assaulted wants to press charges, but I talked him out of it."

"Thank you, Sheriff Cabot."

"Don't mention it, but you owe him a weekend at the ranch."

Ross managed a tight smile. "We can handle it. Just give us the name and we will take care of it."

"What do you want me to do about Junior?"

"Let him spend another night in jail to cool off. Someone will come get him in the morning."

"Will do."

"What was that about Junior?" Franklin Sr. asked, coming from the library.

"He's in jail," Ross answered.

"Jail? What for?"

"Drunk, battery, and disorderly," Ross answered. "The usual. He's fine. I told Sheriff Cabot to let him cool it off in jail another night."

Franklin Sr. worried expression slipped. "Junior getting drunk, you guys fighting over some woman." He shook his head. "Things are getting out of hand."

"I do not want to talk about this," Ross quipped. Silence fell between father and son.

"Well, at least Junior is all right."

Ross felt guilty. He was sure Junior had gotten drunk because of the situation with Nikki. He headed toward the door.

"Ross?" his father caller after him.

Ross refocused on his father, a blank look on his face. He was not in the mood to hear another lecture.

"Good luck on the event," Franklin Sr. said out of the blue, and walked off without another word.

Ross stood for a moment in disbelief. He couldn't remember the last time his father had wished him luck before an event.

"You should go and talk to him," Corina urged. "Anyone can see you guys care about each other."

"How could you know something like that?" She packed the rest of her clothing, then zipped the suitcase.

"Because it was faith that brought you here." Corina reached out and grabbed her hands. "The feelings between you two is obvious."

Nikki removed her hands from hers. "There is no future for us. You saw how he was acting today. It's over. Hell, it never got started." She placed her hands on her hips. "I'm leaving in the morning."

"In the morning?" Corina said in surprise. "What? We just got here. What about the rodeo?"

"I'm not going," Nikki said.

"I think you are giving up too easily," Corina said. "If I knew that you were going to run off, we could have stayed in D.C. Running away isn't the answer."

"I'm not running away," Nikki said. "I'm just continuing on a trip I was already on. And this is the best vacation spot in the country. You and the kids will love it."

Corina stood. "Sounds like a cop out to me."

Nikki shrugged. "Whatever. Why don't you get out of here, enjoy the ranch, and let me finish packing? I will give you a quick tour."

Corina took a deep breath out of frustration. "Why not? I'm not getting anywhere here. I'll see you later."

Nikki shooed her out. "Go. Your husband and boys are probably wondering where you are."

The next morning, Nikki awakened to a loud knocking on the door. Startled, she sat up straight. The knocking continued. Half asleep, she trekked to the door. She opened it and came face to face with David. He was leaning in the doorway, eating an apple. He pushed the large cowboy hat back on his head.

"Why are you up so early?" She turned on her heels and headed back in the room.

David followed. "Folks get up early around these parts."

Nikki stretched. "Tell me about it. I thought doctors kept odd hours, but we have nothing on these cowboys."

"I'm going to be riding to the rodeo with some of the hired hands tomorrow."

"How did you swing that?"

"I hung out with some of the boys last night," David said.

"Don't tell me, they took you to The Big Boot?"

"Yeah! You know it. I had the time of my life."

"I've been there," Nikki said. "That line dance is no joke." Nikki disappeared into the bathroom. She splashed cold water on her face, quickly dressed, and ran a comb through her long, black hair.

David took a seat in the chair. He crossed one long leg over the other.

Nikki gathered up her hair and pulled it into a ponytail. "What time are you guys headed out?"

David glanced at his watch. It was 7:00 a.m. "In about an hour. We're to get everything ready for tomorrow."

There was an awkward silence between them.

"You'll get a chance to see Ross ride."

"What about you?"

"What about me?"

"You're the reason I came to RFK," David said. "It's not right for you to just leave like this."

"I know. I'm sorry about that. Like I told Corina, I need to get on the road." She grabbed the suitcase. "My family is waiting for me."

David placed his hands atop hers. "Nikki, I need to know that you're going to be okay."

"I'm fine," Nikki said with a straight face. "Why does everyone keep asking me that?"

"Because everyone is worried about you," David said. "I wish you would stay."

"I can't stay."

"Why not?"

"It's complicated."

"It's complicated only if you make it."

"I cannot explain it," Nikki said. "You just have to take my word for it." She grabbed the handle and rolled the luggage out the door.

"Have you ever seen Ross compete?" David asked, falling into step with her.

"No. I have only seen him ride," Nikki replied. "Ross and I have been like oil and vinegar since I crashed into that stupid fence. I was a fool to think that there could be anything between us."

"From what I saw, I believe that you guys can work it out," David said. "It's not going to be the same without you around here."

"What do you mean?"

"I mean that I had a long talk with Dr. Baker last night."

"And?"

"And he asked me to be his replacement at the Gallop Clinic."

Nikki's eyes stretched. "What?" She squealed. "You weren't even in the running."

"I know. Out of curiosity. I went over to check out the clinic. Dr. Baker was there. We began talking and one thing led to another. The next thing I knew he was offering me the job."

Nikki threw her arms around his neck. She jumped up and down in excitement. "I'm so happy for you. You're going to take it?"

"Damn right I am. This is the chance of a lifetime."

"What about Bayside? Your patients?" Nikki asked.

"Things are changing at Bayside and not for the better. I need a change, and this may be just what the doctor ordered," he joked. "I have to give two-weeks notice, but this feels right for me."

"Well, I'm proud of you. You were here one day and got a new job. I don't know what to say except I'm glad things worked out for you."

"The same thing happened to you, if you want to get technical. That's why you have to stay. We could work together here, just like we did at Bayside."

"I admit that would be awesome. But—"

"But you're leaving." David sighed. "All right, if I can't talk you out of it." He took her suitcase. "Your mind is made up?"

"It is."

"You have a position here if you want it." David took her in his big strong arms and gave her a tight squeeze. He held her so tight she squirmed.

"David, I'm only going up the road. You can come visit."

"That hug should hold you until we see each other again." He returned her suitcase, gave a wave, and walked away.

* * *

"Ready to go?" Dr. Baker asked, walking toward the front door.

"Yeah, I'm all set."

"Are you going to say goodbye to Ross? Junior? Or are you just going to sneak away like a thief in the night?"

"I am not sneaking."

"What do you call it?" Dr. Baker asked.

"You were there the other night," Nikki said. "So, you know Ross and I have nothing left to discuss."

"From what I heard, you have a lot to discuss."

Nikki shook her head. "I want to thank you for everything. I really had a blast working at the Gallop."

"You're welcome. I'm going to miss you, Dr. Phillips." Dr Baker gave a hug.

"David told me the good news," Nikki said." He's your successor."

"Yes. No one else wanted the job," he joked.

Nikki chuckled. "I do not believe that."

"No, he's more than qualified for the position. He will do fine."

"I know he will. I can't think of a better person for the job," Nikki boasted. "But he has some big shoes to fill."

She looked over Dr. Baker's shoulder to see Mabelle, Lilly, and Blake headed toward her. They said their goodbyes. She tried not to cry, but just the thought of not seeing them again caused her to shed a tear. She could not believe how close they'd gotten in just a short time.

"I heard you were leaving," a familiar voice said from behind her. The people parted like the Red Sea. "I can't say I'm sorry to see you go," Lena said.

"I'm going to miss you too, Lena."

"You're not staying for the Invitational?" Lena asked with a smirk.

"No, I'm not. You don't have to worry." Nikki unlocked the car and placed the luggage in the trunk. She jumped in the driver's seat and glanced one last time at Lena before starting the car.

She drove to the end of the street when Ross's truck came out of nowhere. He blocked her path with his vehicle and jumped out. She gulped. She felt butterflies in her stomach.

"Get out of the car," Ross cried. "We need to talk."

Nikki slowly got out of the vehicle. "Ross don't make a scene. We said everything that we needed to say the other night."

"You weren't going to say goodbye?"

"I don't like goodbyes."

"Are you really going to leave like this?"

"Like what?"

"Childish," Ross answered.

"Childish?" Nikki answered in disbelief. "That's funny, coming from you. I'm not the one who used his brother as an excuse to end things between us."

"I made a mistake," Ross confessed. He placed a hand to his chest. He closed the small gap between them. "I know that now. I'm sorry," he said with sincerity. "I don't want you to leave."

Nikki swallowed the lump in her throat. Ross was saying everything that she wanted to hear. She was not sure that she wanted to stay.

"Will you stay with me?" Ross asked.

Nikki opened her mouth to speak, but nothing came out.

"Nikki," Ross prompted. "Can you do that?"

"Ross, I…" she began. "I don't know."

"What do you mean, you don't know?" Ross inquired.

"I need time to think."

"You were sure the other night. Today you need time to think. What is going on, Nikki?"

"I don't know."

"You know what, just forget about it," Ross exclaimed. "I wouldn't want you to strain a brain muscle *thinking*. You want to go, then go." He jumped back in the truck and burned rubber down the street.

Nikki stood there flabbergasted. She watched as the brake lights vanished from view and out of her life.

* * *

Nikki drove through the familiar town of Montgomery. It had changed in five years. There were new homes and businesses on every block. She looked at the clock radio; she made it in under four hours. The time had flown by. She didn't realize it until she saw the Welcome sign. Her mind had been on Ross. He poured his feelings out to her. She was not expecting him to ask her to stay with him. Deep down in her heart, she wanted to stay with him forever, but she didn't want to come between him and his brother. Now that she was gone, they would be able to work things out.

She smiled when she realized that she was on the street where she grew up. Memories from long ago began rushing back. James Avenue still looked the same. A moment later, she stopped in front of 1171. The split-level white frame house still looked the same, except there was an added room on the back of it. There were several vehicles parked out front.

A middle-aged woman rushed out the door with a black cape draped around her neck and large pink rollers in her head. She hurried to her car. "It's a beauty shop," Nikki said to herself. She parked behind the vehicle and got out. She strolled over to the woman searching for something in the backseat of the car.

"Excuse me," Nikki said. The woman seemed flustered.

She was tossing objects in frustration. "Is this a beauty shop?" she asked.

Then she heard her father's voice behind her. "Nicole Olivia Phillips. Is that you?" He pulled her in his arms. He held her so tight that she began to squirm.

"Daddy, I can't breathe."

"It's okay. I'm your father." He stepped back, looking her up and down, a sloppy grin on his face. "You're still as pretty as ever."

Nikki returned his smile. She tucked a strand of dark hair behind her ear. "Stop it, Dad; you're making me blush."

"I'm just telling the truth."

"Dad, it's so good to see you." She hugged him again "Didn't Mom tell you I was coming?"

"She mentioned it," her father said. "I didn't believe her. Five years is too long for you not to come home to see your family." He guided her toward the house.

"I know, Dad. It's just... Mom and I..." Her voice trailed off. "You don't have to tell me. I have had a ringside seat to many of your fights. I have been married to your mother almost forty years. You don't have to tell me about her, but that's no excuse for you to stay away so long." He rubbed her arm up and down in a comforting manner. "We miss you around here."

Nikki bobbed her head up and down as they reached the door of the shop.

"When did Mom open a beauty shop? She never mentioned it on the phone."

"You know your mother; she always enjoyed doing hair, so she talked me into adding this room onto the house."

"Talked you into it?" Nikki chuckled.

"More like demanded."

"That is not the style for you," she heard her mother say to a customer when they walked inside the shop. There were two women under the hair dryer and one in a chair, reading a magazine.

Sophie stopped talking in mid-sentence when she spotted her. She grinned, rushed over, and gave her daughter a hug. "You made it." She looked her up and down. "You look tired." She pulled her further inside. "Get in here. Everybody, this is my daughter, Nicole. She's a doctor," she bragged.

"Nicole, it's nice to see you."

"Hi, Nikki."

"Hi."

Nikki waved. She looked into her mother's misty eyes. She was proud and happy to see her. She had to admit, it felt good to be home.

One Month Later

"How long are you going to mope around here?" Sophie asked one morning at breakfast. She washed and placed a dish in the rack. "It's been a month, and you still haven't found a job."

Nikki finished the last of the orange juice. She walked over and placed the empty glass in the sink. Her father opened the newspaper wider. He learned over the years to tune his wife's nagging out.

"It's not that I haven't found one, I haven't found one that I want to accept."

"Oh, is that all," Sophie said with sarcasm. "Dr. Calhoun over at Memorial Hospital told me they could get you on."

"I said, Mom, I haven't decided."

Sophie dried her hands on her "Kiss The Mom" apron. "It looks like you didn't think things through when you left Bayside."

"You know why I left Bayside," Nikki argued.

"If I told you once, I told you twice—" Sophie began.

"Sophie," her husband exclaimed. "That's enough. Leave the girl alone."

Nikki took that time to make a hasty exit from the room and hurried outside. She sat on the front steps. Raising her knees up, she wrapped her arms around them. Why did she still allow her mother to get to her? The scolding reminded her of when she was a little girl who could never do anything right in her mother's eyes. She was a successful doctor, but she still felt as if she couldn't measure up to her expectations.

The soft tap of her father's finger on her shoulder interrupted her thoughts. He dropped down next to her. "This is where you always come whenever you were upset. It's still your spot."

"Yeah, still my place." She looked up into her dad's kind face. He was a meek and gentle man. The opposite of her mother. She loved her. She just couldn't take her constant nagging.

"In her way, your mother is just trying to help."

"She has a funny way of showing it. She gets on my nerves."

Her father carefully glanced over at her. "Your mother just feels that if you went back to work it would be good for you."

"I know she's right," Nikki replied.

"It will keep your mind off whoever it is that you're trying to forget."

Nikki tilted her head to one side. "There is no one."

"My dear, I heard you on the phone, talking to your friend Corina. He works on the ranch where you did community service. Sounds like you fell for him." Her father raised an eyebrow. "What's his name? What does he do?"

"Were you eavesdropping again?"

"Yes, I was eavesdropping but not on purpose," he said. "Spill it."

"Okay. His name is Ross Kincaid. His family owns the RFK Guest Ranch in Norstrom. He is a three times National Rodeo Champion."

"So, he's a cowboy?"

"Yes. A professional cowboy." Nikki couldn't help but smile. She had thought about him day and night since she left a month ago. She thought he would show up on her doorstep. She hasn't received a phone call or text from Ross. Nothing. She read in the Norstrom Newspaper that he won the Invitational.

"You love him?"

"I believe I do," she answered without hesitation. "I miss him."

"Then why are you here?"

"I'm visiting my family."

"Visit? You have been here a month. You're running."

"It's complicated." Nikki stood. She brushed the dirt from the back of her pants.

"Does he feel the same about you?"

"He asked me to stay with him."

"But?"

"I think it's too late now."

"It is never too late for true love." Her father stood. He placed his arms around her. She leaned her head on his shoulder. "If Ross feels the same about you as you do him, then that's where you should be and not here."

She hugged her father. "Thank you, Daddy."

"You're welcome, pumpkin." He squeezed her tight. "Now, tell me more about this Ross fella."

* * *

The next day, Nikki strolled into the lobby of South East Hospital in downtown Montgomery. It was not as big as Bayside, but it was a licensed acute-care facility. The doors had opened in 1980. It had a state-of-the-art surgery and Orthopedist department for in and outpatients. She looked at the directory. The office of Dr. Joe Calhoun, chief of orthopedics, was located on the 5th floor. She hurried over to the elevators and pushed the up button. She got off, made a right, and headed down the short hall full of offices. A moment later, she was standing in front of 514A. She took a deep breath and knocked on the door. It'd been years since she'd been on an interview. She was nervous. But the biggest surprise was there was a woman seated behind the desk.

"Nikki," the middle-aged, African-American woman said, coming to her feet. She extended a hand.

Nikki blinked. "I'm surprised."

Dr. Calhoun chuckled. "You were expecting a man."

"The name threw me off."

"Don't worry about it. Joe is short for Josephine."

"Different. I like it."

"Please have a seat." Dr. Calhoun pointed to the chair across from her desk. "I was just going over your resume that your mother sent to me."

"My mother?"

"Yes, Mrs. Phillips can be very persuasive," Dr. Calhoun said. "She asked me to look at your resume."

"I'm sorry."

"Don't be. I know all about strong-willed mothers. I have one myself." She refocused on the resume. "But I'm glad I did. I'm impressed. Graduated in the top five of your class, over five hundred surgeries, and surgeon of the year. Lots of awards and accolades here."

"Thank you."

"We would love to have you on staff. But we aren't a large medical center like Bayside. With your experience and credentials, you can work anywhere."

"This is my home. I was born and raised here," she explained. Then her cellular phone rang. "I'm sorry, I thought I had it on vibrate." She reached inside the bag to retrieve it. She glanced at the number to see that the call was from Blake. Her first instinct was not to answer until after the interview, but Blake would not call unless it was important. "Dr. Calhoun, I need to take this. Can I step out a moment?"

"Why don't you take it here? I'll go get a cup of coffee."

"Thank you," Nikki said. She quickly answered the call. "Blake, what is it? I was right in the middle—"

"It's Ross," Blake said in shaken tone.

"Ross?" Nikki exclaimed. "What's wrong? Is he all right?"

"He was tossed by a bull," Blake said. "It's pretty bad."

Nikki's heart felt like it was smashed into a million pieces.

She imagined the worst. "Is he…" The rest of the sentence died on her lips.

"No, he's at the Clinic."

"The Gallop?"

"Yes, he's there until he's stable enough to be transferred to the medical center in Houston."

"Give me the details," Nikki replied. She ran out of the room, passing Dr. Calhoun on the way in. "I have to go. I'll call you," she shouted over her shoulder.

* * *

Twenty minutes later, Nikki rushed inside the house. She headed upstairs to her bedroom and inside the closet. She grabbed her luggage, opened it, and began tossing clothes inside. She prayed all the way for Ross to be okay. "The fool," she said to herself. "He knew the risk but still chose to get on that stupid bull. I'm going to kill him when I see him…" She moved into the bathroom and grabbed the overnight bag.

"What's going on?" Sophie exclaimed, coming into the room. She stopped dead in her tracks when she noticed her daughter packing. "Dr. Calhoun said something about a 911 call. What is this about?"

Nikki looked over her shoulder to see her father following her mother. "Ross?"

"Yes, I have to go to Norstrom."

"What for?" her mother asked with a bewildered look on her face. "What about Dr. Calhoun? I don't believe this. I worked hard to get you that interview and this is how you repay me? By running out?"

"Mother, I don't have time for this." She grabbed the bags and headed for the door.

"You'd better make time."

"Sophie, give it a rest," her father chimed in.

A look of surprise flashed across her mother's face. "Honey," she crooned.

"Pumpkin, what is this about? Did something happen to Ross?"

"He was injured during a ride. I'm going back to Norstrom."

"Hold on a second, who is Ross?" her mother asked, looking from husband to daughter.

"I don't have time to explain." Nikki rushed out the door, down the stairs, and out to the car. She opened the driver-side door and slid behind the wheel.

"Would you like for me to drive you?" her father suggested, coming around to the driver's side. "You don't look so good."

"Well, I—"

"Scoot over." He hopped in the front seat. "Sophie, I'll call you later, when we get there."

"No, you won't. I'm going, too. I want to know who this Ross is." She jumped in the backseat of the car.

"What about your shop?" Nikki asked.

"It'll be fine," Sophie said. "Let's go."

✳ ✳ ✳

Hours later, the car pulled up in front of the Gallop Clinic. Nikki jumped out of the vehicle and ran inside the building. No one was at the desk. The staff had gone for the day. She looked around frantically for someone to give her information on Ross.

Nikki," she heard David call.

"How is he?" Nikki asked in a frantic tone.

"He reinjured his spine. It's swollen. There's no feeling in his legs."

Nikki gasped. "You won't know anything for sure until the swelling goes down."

"Exactly. He's one lucky cowboy," David replied. "It could have been worse."

"Can I see him?"

"Of course," David said. "He's in exam room B."

Nikki turned to leave.

"Nikki, it's good to see you again," David said. "You look good."

Nikki hurried to the exam room. She strolled in to find Blake, Junior, and Franklin Sr. by his bedside.

Junior zoomed over to her. "What the hell are you doing here?"

"Pipe down, Junior," Blake replied. "I called her."

"What? Why? She's the reason he was injured."

"That's nonsense and you know it," Blake replied.

"I had to come." Nikki said.

"And you jumped in your car and rushed to check on him," Junior said in a sarcastic tone.

She had not seen Junior since their last conversation at the manor. He was still angry at her.

"I said give it a rest, boy." Franklin Sr. voice boomed. "I had Blake call her here."

Junior pointed at Nikki. "He may not ever ride again because of her."

"What are you talking about? What did I do?"

"You roped my brother in, broke his heart, and ran out on him. He never should have been on that bull. His mind has not been on riding since you left. You even had me fooled."

"Junior, this isn't about you," Franklin Sr. said.

"It's too early to determine whether he is able to ride again," David explained. "We have to wait until the swelling goes down to know the extent of the damage."

Nikki walked over and stood next to the bed. She looked lovingly down at Ross.

"Do you love my son?" Franklin Sr. asked. "That is the reason why you came"

The question threw Nikki off guard. She had to be honest about her feelings for Ross. "Yes, I do." She reached down and took his hand in hers. Ross needed her. She was going to stay by his side. No matter the outcome or what anyone said. She reached out and stroked the side of his cheek. "Where else would I be but by his side? No matter what. I love him."

"That's all I needed to hear," Franklin Sr. said. "What about you, boys?"

"Sounds good to me," Blake agreed.

"I think she should have her head examined," Junior sing-songed. "I still think she's with the wrong brother."

"Junior," Franklin Sr. chastised.

"I love you, too," Nikki heard a voice say in a raspy tone.

She looked down to see Ross's beautiful brown eyes looking back at her. "What the—" She attempted to remove her hand, but he held it tighter.

Ross took her hand and held it against his face. "What took you so long to get here?"

"How long have you been awake?"

"The whole time," David answered. Her parents strolled in the room.

Nikki glanced around the room. They all looked like the cat that swallowed the canary. "Will someone tell me what is going on here?"

Ross sat up straight. He scooted up to the head of the bed. "What's going on is." He threw the covers back, swung his long legs over the side, and stood.

Nikki's mouth gaped. "You're not hurt?"

"Only my heart."

"Are you Ross?" Sophie demanded. "The one who broke my little girl's heart?"

"You must be Dr. Phillips' parents," Franklin Sr. said.

"We must be, I'm Sophie Phillips and this is my husband, George. Who are you?"

"I'm Franklin. Kincaid, Sr. These are my sons, Blake and Junior. And my boy Ross did not break anyone's heart. It was the other way around."

"I don't think so," Sophie threw in. "My daughter is sweet, kind, and considerate. She did not hurt anyone. She is a doctor for Christ sake."

While they argued, Nikki's and Ross's eyes locked.

"I'm sorry, Nikki. This was the only way that I could think of to get you here."

"You could have come to Montgomery."

"I was afraid of getting the door slammed in my face. The way I treated you the last time we saw each other, I didn't think you would see me."

"Isn't that how we met?"

Ross reached out and took her hand in his. "I admit things have been intense between us since the beginning. I think that's what attracted me to you. But I have to know, did you mean what you said about loving me?"

"Yes, I did," Nikki said. "I do love you, very much."

Ross covered the small space between them. He placed his forehead on hers. "Then let me ask you once more," he said. "Stay with me."

"Come on." Blake and Junior cut into their conversation.

"Is that all you got?" Junior continued. "If you don't ask her to marry you then I will."

Ross sighed. He dropped his head and tilted it to one side. "Stay out of this, Junior."

Nikki looked at Ross and smiled. "Is that what you want to ask me, Ross?"

His mouth gaped. "Eventually. I—"

"You don't have to explain," Nikki said. "How about we slow it down, just a little. Get to really know each other."

Ross took her hand in his. "That is exactly what I was thinking." They looked over to see everyone staring at them.

"Why don't we go somewhere and talk about it?" Nikki said.

"Why don't we?" Ross led her out of the room.

"What do you mean by taking it slow?" Sophie asked the couple as they passed her.

"How long is it going to take? I have to get started on planning the wedding," she continued. "It should be in Montgomery."

"What are you talking about, woman?" Franklin Sr. chimed in. "It's going to be here on the ranch."

"The hell you say?" Nikki heard her mother say as she and Ross walked out of the clinic and under the moonlit stars.

Ross leaned over and gave her a kiss. "How about a ride underneath the stars?"

Nikki arched an eyebrow. "I'm game. You do owe me a ride."

THE END

About The Author

Sammie Ward is an Author/Writer/ Publisher who was born and raised in North Little Rock, Arkansas, and now residing in Maryland. She began writing Confessions short stories on the advice of a friend. Since then, she has written over sixty short stories, six novels, and one novella. To learn more about Sammie Ward. Visit her website: https://www.ladyleopublishing.com.

Also From Sammie Ward

Novels

Quarter To Midnight (The Victor Sexton Series) Book 2

A Little Hot Chocolate For My Soul (Anthology)

Lace & Honor (LoveStorm Romance)

Love To Behold (Novella)

It's In The Rhythm (Indigo)

7 Days (The Victor Sexton Series) Book 1

In The Name of Love (LoveStorm Romance)

Short Stories

Joseph The Dreamer

David The Shepherd Boy

Ruth the Faithful

A Touch of Magic

What Are Girlfriends For?

The Sweetest Thing

When Love Comes Around

A Line In The Sand

Weekend Escapade

Second Chance At Love

Sweet Island Temptation

Smooth Operator

www.ingramcontent.com/pod-product-compliance
Lightning Source LLC
Chambersburg PA
CBHW030641110726
47901CB00002B/527